Trapped!

The darkness lifted suddenly, along with the metal roof above her head. Kelly blinked a couple of times in the bright light, her stressed brain finally grasping that she was trapped in a car trunk. Panic threatened again as she realized she could be anywhere. She might never be found.

There was a man looking down at her, rough looking, raw around the edges. His eyes open wide with a frantic look, the look someone gets when backed into a corner by a wild bear, like he had no choice but to shoot or be eaten. Kelly would not have been surprised to see foam at his mouth. She looked for it, but she saw instead the raw determination of the set of his lips. Naturally thin, they were like two narrow straight lines pinched together.

Spittle accompanied the words as he spoke.

"Ah, I thought you would be awake. Too bad I can't say the same thing for your friend over there." He laughed a little, a mad, insane laugh

By Lara Steele

Romance
Tender Bait

Fantasy
Ice Fire

Tender Bait

by Lara Steele

Lazy Tales • Seattle

Tender Bait
is a Lazy Tales book

First Edition 2015

Available from Amazon.com
and other book stores

Available on Kindle
and other devices

LazyTales.com

Thanks Merelee

For the example you set

Prologue

Crouched in the protection of the woods the shadow cloaked figure waited. He peered through a spotting scope at the grisly scene below. What he saw sickened him, though he knew his own actions had caused it.

His thoughts drifted. He closed his eyes; only for a moment. The scene played before him. All he could see was his own face, thankfully not what had been done. The smile on his deeply cragged face was beautiful to behold. There was only an edge of madness to it. No one deserved that kind of happiness. He reveled in the feel of it. Joy bordering on insani....no, not that word...on ecstasy. Yes, ecstasy. Grinning now, the dark man opened his eyes.

The sinister man shifted the spotting scope, very slightly. He watched as a woman bounced along the trail, laughing with her friend. Adjacent to the tree she stopped. He was too far away to hear her scream, but he saw her throw her hands to her mouth in shock as her partner tried to comfort her.

The man watched. These two were not of that much interest to him. The one he wanted would come, if he was just patient. It wouldn't be long now. She would come and he would be ready.

Chapter One

"Oh, great, he's spewing his guts," Jack Hall muttered under his breath. Jack's newbie partner was bent over as Hall walked up. Jack was not pleased. Great, just great! Not only do they stick me with a new partner, but this one can't even handle a double homicide.

It looked like his new partner had eaten breakfast before coming to the scene; definitely the sign of a beginner. Right after Jack laid down the rules, letting him know who the senior detective was, he would also cover when not to eat. No one in this line of work ever ate before going to a murder scene, at least not more than once. He thought as a grim smile came to his face.

Jack was totally disgusted by the situation. His new partner, Kelly Swift, was supposed to meet him at the murder scene, but Jack had expected to find Kelly standing there taking notes. Instead he found Kelly bent over double and heaving up breakfast. To top it off, the guy had poor taste in clothes. Kelly's pants were a light khaki colored slacks material. They hugged the butt, and flared out a little at the bottom. The jacket was tailored to fit, but due to his tiny waist it gave him the appearance of hips.

Kelly was small of stature, about 5'5" at the most, judging from what Jack could see at the moment. Also, it looked like Kelly was a wimp. The guy couldn't have been 135 pounds dripping wet. Jack bet Kelly couldn't even lift 100 pounds. In short Kelly's clothes, coupled with his build, made him look gay. How in the world did this Kelly Swift ever make detective? Jack wondered. Why are they saddling me with this?

Kelly felt her guts being torn out as she bent over. All she could think about was those poor women. Kelly hadn't been able to look at them for more than a moment. Even with such a short glance at the bodies, she felt her gorge start to rise, knowing she was about to lose her breakfast. Rushing as far away from the primary crime scene as she could manage, she bent over double and let it come, her stomach cramping.

Having emptied breakfast onto the ground, Kelly stood up. She tucked her hair behind her ears and wiped her mouth surreptitiously on her sleeve. At least she hoped nobody noticed. She was thankful she always carried water with her.

Digging into her jacket pocket she retrieved a bottle of water and took a few long pulls. She couldn't believe her stomach had betrayed her like this, and on her first day of work too! What would Jack think of her when he showed up? Would he even remember her?

Jack was still staring doggedly at his partner's back when the guy finally finished upchucking and stood up. Auburn hair cascaded down past the shoulder blades of the dark blue department issued jacket on her back. Jack hardly noticed when she raised her sleeve to her mouth and wiped it. He was too lost in his own thoughts. Oh, man, Kelly Swift was a girl!

Now it was obvious. Her clothes were perfect for a modern business woman. The shoes maybe a bit too dressy for field work, but Jack supposed that was to be expected. He hadn't gotten much warning about showing up at the scene and he was the senior detective. They would have called him before they called her. She would have been dressing to impress in the office, not to do field work. It was sheer chance that Jack lived close enough to go straight to the scene instead of going into the office first.

His new partner was a woman! Jack thought frantically trying to figure a way out of this mess. This was worse than a wimpy man. His new partner was a girl, fresh on the force. Headquarters must have made a mistake. There was no way he could work with a girl, not after the last partner he had. The captain had made a mistake. Jack was sure a simple phone call would straighten this all out.

Jack pulled out his cell phone and was starting to call his captain, when Kelly turned around and he saw her face for the first time. Jack's hand dropped loosely to his side without finishing the call. Kelly Swift was Kelly Thomas, his amazing one night fling from high school. Immediately upon seeing her face he was transported back to that wonderful, hot, steamy prom night.

Their long stroll through the soft evening light had been unforgettable. She had looked radiant, full of promise. Her short, blue, sleeveless evening gown set off her eyes perfectly—eyes that looked out with trust and longing of their own. Her scent was of fresh lilacs and her skin tasted slightly sweet. Her legs were so long they seemed to go on forever. He had wanted her so badly his body ached.

When at last he had her alone and on her back she responded wonderfully to him. Her body arching up at the slightest touch, asking for more caresses. Her perfect hips, firm and slender. Her breasts soft and full in the light of the moon, the way they felt when his hands slowly closed over them. Even now he felt himself react to the thought of her. Jack's hands reflexively opened and closed as if he were back ten years before, with her on that lovely, moonlit night.

His attention was snapped back to the present when his cell phone, forgotten in his hand, dropped painfully onto his toe and tumbled to the dirt trail beside his foot. He almost hopped on one foot, but she distracted him from the pain with a little wave. She started walking his way and he wasn't ready to speak to her yet.

Quickly he bent over to retrieve his phone from the ground. He used this cover to take a deep breath and compose his face back to something less awestruck. At least he hoped he looked pleasantly surprised and not totally blown away when he stood up to meet her eyes with his own.

"Hi, Jack," Kelly's radiant smile still transformed her face from nice and comfortable to beautiful and exotic.

Jack was at a loss for words for a moment, he found his eyes dropping to her breasts. They had certainly filled out very nicely in the last ten years. It took all his will power to bring his eyes back up to her face.

All the things he was going to say to his new partner were suddenly gone. He had planned how he would explain what happened to his old partner, what the ground rules were for the partnership and what he expected in a new partner. Jack couldn't remember any of it. The shock of seeing Kelly again drove that right out of his head.

Jack finally managed, "Uh, Kelly… Swift?" He said the last name with a question and an emphasis that suggested she should explain. He truly knew there could be no explanation. She had forgotten him, or at least moved on and gotten married, while he had…what? Hoped that someday he would find someone as wonderful as she was?

Seeing her again made him realize that was what he had been doing. Waiting for someone to come along who would measure up to Kelly Thomas and their wonderful one night stand. It was equally obvious, since she had gotten married, she hadn't waited for him.

"Yeah, it's a long story," Kelly was trying to sound blasé, but Jack read some very deep emotions in her eyes. "I can fill you in sometime." He wondered what that was all about. Kelly had finished high school and moved to Washington State to go to college. He had stayed and gone to the University of Colorado in Boulder, their hometown. He had not heard from her since that first semester. He had no idea she had moved back.

Years ago he had come to grips with her forgetting about him. Or so he thought. Jack had known, even at eighteen years old, that what they had was special. He would never be able to forget about her. She was still the only woman he had ever loved. After she left, he had buried himself in his studies at school and his work. Sometimes he had even buried himself in other things.

He had taken other lovers, but never loved the women who shared his bed. He could plainly see she had not had the same problem moving on that he had. She had fallen in love, married and it looked like life had been kind to her. Other than a slight crease in between her eyes there were no worry lines. In fact he thought he saw a few laugh lines in the tan that colored her face.

The secretive man was disappointed when another detective joined the auburn haired beauty. He stood between the scope and the woman. The man didn't want to look at the intruder's broad shoulders. The woman was much more to his liking.

He watched for a few more moments as they talked. Shifting on the ground he willed the man to move. His palms itched to see her again. His thoughts....no he would wait to savor her reaction to meeting him. He could almost feel her soft hand in his own, shaking his hand, not realizing until it was too late the surprise he had in store for her, especially for her. A soft moan escaped his closed lips.

He wanted to be the one talking to her, or doing other things. He adjusted his pants as the thought of getting her alone overwhelmed him. The things he would learn would be invaluable. He would watch. Maybe the other detective would leave her alone long enough for him to get his answers. The smile on his face was feral, but not as savage as the long low chuckle coming from deep in his chest.

Chapter Two

Jack was at a loss to understand how Kelly had just dropped back into his life. Several questions popped into his mind, none of which had anything to do with the two dead women tied to the tree in front of him. With great difficulty he dragged his concentration and his eyes back to the tree, and more importantly the two women there.

The first thing he noticed was the clothes. Clothes told him a lot about the murder victim. They gave a good detective something to go on, as far as determining the social class of the victim. Knowing this he could figure out what kind of places they hung out, if they were college students, professionals, or even bums.

If he could figure that out, he could infer what type of person the murderer would probably be. Something about this double homicide just didn't add up. For one thing, it didn't look like there had been a struggle. For another whoever these women were, they were obviously fashion conscious, and on the fast track with their careers.

This meant that they hung out at high class establishments. They had good paying jobs and were not likely college students. They probably didn't go to the low class establishments, but rather visited the nicer bars. Yes, he was sure he would never find them at The Dive, the topless bar out on the edge of town. No, they would stay with the nice bars on Pearl Street, if they even went out to the bars at all.

Jack shifted his attention from the victims' clothes to their facial features. It was then that Jack realized why Kelly had been so upset. Both women really looked like her. Not in the way twins do, but more like sisters would, slightly younger sisters. They had the same flowing auburn hair, the same blue eyes, the nice clothes, even the shoes were similar. He could imagine the perfect white teeth and spunky little nose that would have been there if there had not been a gaping hole instead.

Jack was running through all the possible murder weapons, but he thought it must have been a gun with a hollow point bullet at very close range. A large caliber at that, or the hollow point would have shattered in the head and never made it out the other side.

"What kind of sick person could have done this?" Kelly asked. She tucked a loose strand of hair behind one ear, a habit she had when nervous. She had been totally unprepared for what she would find when she left for work that morning. Then throwing up right before she met her new partner... old boyfriend... incredible lover that she could never forget... whatever he was. That had totally put her off balance. She was scrambling for something to say and she knew it.

To Kelly, Jack looked totally cool, and impeccably dressed, just as she remembered. Today his immaculately pressed sport coat was made of rich grey wool. His pants matched the coat, but instead of a dress shirt and tie he wore a solid blue t-shirt. The whole combination managed to give him a rugged look. The relaxed waves of his hair were brushed over to one side and not a hair was out of place.

He looked yummy enough to eat. His tan made it look like he was just back from a nudist colony in Hawaii. Jack nude. Oh, that was not a thought she needed to pursue right now, no matter how much she wanted to. Instead she turned her attention to his face. He was a little taller and broader in the shoulders than he had been in high school. None of him was going to flab.

The strong lines of his jaw had not at all diminished over the last ten years. She wondered if he had gone on to play college football. If so, what had sent him on the path of law enforcement instead of into the family ranching business or professional football? Maybe she would have a chance to ask him later.

There was so much she wanted to catch up on. Only some of those things involved talk. She had to stop thinking that way. She had no idea if he was married, dating, or even if he remembered that night long ago.

She hadn't talked to him since she had met her late husband, Paul. Her one and only letter to Jack, from college, had been a month after she got there. It had never been returned. Kelly had fallen for Paul the second semester of her freshman year at Washington State University. Studying criminal justice, from the perspective of a paralegal, didn't give her much time for social pursuits. She wasn't sure why she had even gone out with Paul. Only now did she realize that her relationship with Paul had been a desperate attempt to fill the hole left by the man standing in front of her.

Jack had turned to look squarely at the two women hanging in the tree. Kelly remembered his beautiful blue eyes. She looked for them now in his strong profile. He seemed to look right through the crime scene and yet take in everything at once. He was just standing there studying the scene. She wondered what he could be gathering from just looking at the scene. How could he be so calm? In a small college town like Boulder, murder was not that common, particularly not murders like this.

Kelly was shocked at the thought that a few years ago, one of those girls could have been her. Her first choice in careers hadn't done much to prepare her for this kind of work. Looking at crime from a desk, as a paralegal, wasn't as in your face as this.

Kelly wasn't sure what to do, but didn't want to interrupt Jack. "I think I'll go talk to the hikers who found the bodies."

"Uh, huh," Jack was non-committal for a moment. He seemed to wake up from his daze and continued, "While you are at it, try to canvass a few of the houses near the trailhead. People that live near the Flatirons are used to quiet nights. Someone may have noticed a struggle and still be home."

There were a lot of responses that Kelly entertained, like saying something she would regret, such as 'I grew up here,' or 'I may be new to the force, but I'm not stupid,' or 'let's ditch this and get a room.' What came out of her mouth instead was a thin "Sure, Jack" before clamping it shut. Pressing her lips tight together, she strode off to do as she was told.

The threatening man set down the scope and considered his options. Charging down the hill, coat flapping, demanding her attention was obviously out, but the thought brought a light chuckle to his lips. Clamping down on it he forced himself to concentrate. How was he to snare her? How long would he need to wait? Could he wait? Pondering, working through the distractions in his mind, the man realized he was laughing, a high pitched nasally sound. Exerting great mental effort, jerking his mind back to the present, he clinched down on the sound.

After a long time he picked up the scope again. The woman had left the man and was working her way through the crowd, as if that would save her. She was wrong. From his vantage point he could see for miles. She would not escape him.

Chapter Three

Jack watched Kelly carefully. Maybe that tight set to her mouth didn't really mean she was upset with him. Maybe she was just shaken at the sight of so much blood. It really was a brutal sight. How on earth did sweet Kelly Thomas wind up as a detective in homicide? How did she wind up with Swift as a last name? When did she get married? The part of him that was glad she had found someone to share her life with was at war with the part that just wanted another hot and steamy night.

What was he thinking? Of course he was glad she was married. Partnering unmarried, opposite sex cops together was just asking for trouble. He would never, ever put a relationship before his job again. He shuddered a bit; the last time he dated someone else on his police force it ended badly. Not wanting to think about it, he turned his attention back to the crime scene.

Being careful not to touch the bodies, he searched the ground for clues that the murderer might have left behind.

Chautauqua Park was home to the Flatirons and miles of hiking trails. Several hundred people used this park daily. It was unlikely that he would find anything significant, but he knew he had to look.

The tree the two women were in had shed its leaves, covering the ground for a good 15 feet all around the trunk. Everywhere he looked bright red, orange and faint greens covered up the ground. Jack couldn't see the soil well and he didn't dare disturb the leaves to search more thoroughly before the forensic guys got there. He even had to be careful where he stepped. There was no way he was going to mess up clues and let this guy get away.

Finally, giving up, Jack walked a little away from the tree to where the grass was exposed. There was some trampled grass, but no real foot prints. This fall, the snows were late and the ground was hard and dry. He would leave the difficult task of searching for hidden clues in the dirt and surrounding area to the experts. He turned his attention back to the bodies, disgusted that he had been so distracted when he first saw them. Seeing Kelly again had really thrown him, but now he was ready to focus on the dead women.

Both women had their hands tied above their heads and were hanging from the tree. Jack noticed missing bark on some higher branches. He surmised the attacker must have used a branch like a pulley. Their assailant would have had to swing the rope over the branch. Tie one end to their hands. Pull them up. Then he secured them to a lower branch; probably the highest one he could reach. This would mean the murderer was about 5'8" tall, shorter than Jack, but taller than the women. He had used rough rope to tie them up. It was old brown rope with some kind of grease on it. Maybe that would give the guys in forensics something to go on.

Each of the victims had one gunshot wound in the head. There was a pool of blood below their feet. There was not much left of their faces so the shot must have come from behind, leaving a larger hole where the exit wound was. The picture that was painted in Jack's mind ran over and over again in a loop. Like a bad video, the attacker dragging the women to the tree, first one, than the other. Tying them up. Hoisting them into the tree. The terrified women hanging there and finally, the gun shot.

It just didn't add up to Jack. This was too public a place. Why didn't someone hear something? This park wasn't that secluded. A gunshot would have been noticed by someone, no matter what time it was.

The victims were wearing nice slacks and blazers but had on tennis shoes. Had they just been out for a stroll? The tennis shoes were incongruent with the rest of their professional wardrobe. They were appropriate for a lunchtime walk, but it was early morning.

Jack had too many questions and not enough answers. He didn't like it at all. If only the killer had given them a little help in identifying the victims, they might figure this out a whole lot faster. As it was without a purse, with nothing in the pockets of their blazers, and with no possible dental records it might take a long time to identify the two women.

Kelly walked to the edge of the police tape, ducked under, and made her way through the spectators gathered there. Many were crowded up to the tape, trying to get a better view. A few stood a little way back trying to take surreptitious glances out of the corner of their eyes. Kelly wondered what they were thinking. She hoped they were grossed out or horrified, but just couldn't fight human nature. It seemed that anytime there was a disaster, people gravitated toward it like a meteorite pulled toward the earth.

Kelly walked up to a nearby black and white response vehicle, a Dodge truck. She slowly approached the young couple sitting on the back tailgate of the truck, wanting to get a good first impression of them. From her courses, Kelly knew that the person who called in the crime was often the one who committed it. However, there was no way this young couple could have been responsible for these murders. She would bet her life on it. They looked too shocked, their faces pale and mouths slightly open.

They were young and clean cut. They gave the appearance of two college students who had been out enjoying the brisk morning air when they had come upon the bodies. They both had on blue jeans and lightweight non-descript jackets.

"Hi, I'm Detective Kelly Swift," she started as she pulled out her notebook and pen. "I understand that you made the initial 911 call reporting this incident. Can I ask you a few questions?"

The girl looked at her friend and when he didn't seem to say anything she took over. "Sure, I called it in, but Sam saw it first."

Sam seemed to be in shock. He sat there staring straight ahead. He didn't even glance toward Kelly. Looking at the girl instead, Kelly asked, "When did you first see the bodies?" It seemed like Kelly was more likely to get answers from the girl instead of the boy.

"Right before we made the 911 call. It was the only thing I could think to do. I mean they were obviously dead already." There was a bit of panic in her voice. "They were, weren't they?" she asked desperately, as if she was afraid they had made a horrible mistake.

"Yes, they were already dead," Kelly reassured her, "you did the right thing." She didn't need the girl freezing on her too. "It's okay. This isn't your fault." Kelly decided that she wasn't going to get much more out of them now, but it was very important to get first impressions before the brain could play tricks with what they remembered. Kelly had been told that memory wasn't very dependable and this explained why witnesses often contradicted each other.

"Did you touch anything in the area?" Kelly continued. The girl didn't answer immediately. "Think hard, did you touch the bodies or the trees?" Kelly watched her closely. After each question the girl shook her head.

"We were laughing and joking as we walked. Neither of us noticed..." she hesitated, face pale. "We didn't see them until we were near those bushes over there," she said, indicating a row of bushes several yards from the bodies. No wonder the guy was in shock. It was a gruesome sight.

Kelly was baffled. Why couldn't she seem to get any real answers out of this couple? Why was the boy still sitting there in shock? It was not going at all like it did in detective school; best to wrap this up before she started to show her frustration. The girl's non-answers were getting annoying.

"Okay. I assume this officer already took your statements?" Kelly asked pointing at the woman in uniform, waiting patiently nearby. At the girl's affirmative nod, Kelly continued, "Then I will let you go on with your day."

"Thank you for all of your help," Kelly took the girl's hand in what she hoped was a comforting manner. "This officer will tell you what to do and give you a number to call if you need anything," Kelly finished, waving the officer over.

Stepping back and looking around, Kelly took inventory of the crowd. There were a couple of clean cut college students and a few kids with purple, spiked hair and artfully gashed jeans. In the background there were three hikers in their lightweight jackets, sporty tops and khaki pants. No one looked like a murderer to Kelly, not that she had a lot of experience yet. She sighed and went to interview them anyway. As she thought, no one in the crowd knew anything. In her opinion, if the murderer had hung around to observe, he was a fantastic actor, deserving of an Oscar. Kelly suspected that he was long gone. She started toward the nearest house about a block down the road.

The sinister man glanced up at the quickly rising sun. He was tired. Shoulders drooping, he scurried back further into the shade, taking his spotting scope with him. Once he was sequestered within the cool shade he settled the scope to his eye again.

At first he panicked. He couldn't find the detective he had been tracking. He jerked the scope in short little movements from side to side, trying to locate her. A small curse escaped his lips when he thought he might not find her at all. Finally, taking a deep breath he focused on the women in the tree again.

Slowly he moved the scope, tracing the ghost of her steps. He could be patient. It would be so much easier to be patient if he weren't so tired. The scope was heavy in his hands. Heavy like the gun had not been. The gun... no, he would not think about the gun. Thinking about the gun would only lead to madness. The gun was only necessary because they had suffered so much.

He had not meant to make them suffer. All he wanted was to feel that joy. The joy that transcended all the hurt in his soul. When he saw that beautiful face in his mind, when he thought of those eyes looking into his pleadingly, it soothed him. Soothed hurts from when he was so young.

Young and innocent. Young and oh, so, vulnerable. So unfair. His hand tightened on the scope. Images flashed through his mind.

A young boy clutching the remains of his bear watching the knife in her hand.

Jump.

The knife in his own hand, blood on the point.

Jump.

The fist coming at his right eye.

Jump.

The feel of her bones cracking under the thrust of his own fist.

Jump.

The time she... NO!

The shout seemed to come from behind his shoulder.

He looked but no one was there. Facing forward again, he realized the scope was digging into the soft fleshy part of his palm. Slowly he loosened his grip in the scope, flexing his fingers. He wanted to put it down, but he was drawn inexplicably toward the woman detective.

The direction she had walked was congested now, even within the police tape. The forensics team had arrived and they were busy examining the scene. He lingered for a moment on one of the more shapely workers, but she wasn't his goal. He moved on, finally catching up to his quarry as she started across the street. She could run, but she would not escape him. He laughed a little under his breath – a sure sign he was tired.

Chapter Four

Jack puzzled over the murder scene as the forensics team arrived. They pulled up in their city issued blue sedan and four of them spilled out. Immediately they set to work, swarming carefully over the scene like ants at a picnic. Instantly the crime scene was transformed from a forest path to some kind of science lab. Everywhere there was a possible clue someone was working or there was a marker down. Suddenly numbered markers appeared everywhere, scattered in a seemingly haphazard way. Jack absently noticed them marking the disturbed area that he had seen earlier in the grass.

Next came the notebooks and the pens. Notes were being made and comments thrown about from one person to the other. Sometimes one investigator would call another over to discuss something they found on the ground. Jack knew the click whir sound of camera shutters would soon follow.

When Jack saw the coroner pull up, followed closely by a silent ambulance, he knew it was time to get going. The forensics team and coroner examinations would take several hours. Jack wanted to demand answers from the coroner right away, but he knew that it would be pointless. The coroner probably wouldn't know anything for a couple of days. The forensics people were likely to be even longer presenting their findings. Jack was getting nowhere standing there.

Unlike the fiction of movies, it actually takes a lot of time to run a DNA test and to get some of the answers this team needed. It was up to him to try to handle the human aspect of the investigation. He had gathered all the clues he could without disturbing the scene. It was time to concentrate on his part of the job.

Despite ordering Kelly to ask the neighbors questions, he wasn't about to let her do it alone. This case would require more experience than a rookie had. He reluctantly admitted to himself that it might even require more experience than he had. He made his way toward the police tape with quick unwavering strides. Ducking under the yellow line that read "DO NOT CROSS," in bold capital letters, he looked for Kelly's shapely curves.

Kelly knew her partner was Jack Hall a full week before she was supposed to start work. She wondered if he hadn't been told. More likely he didn't know she had been married and changed her last name, she reasoned. It certainly had looked like shock on his face when she turned around and he saw her. Of course, she thought, it could have been disgust too. She supposed it was not every day you discover your partner can't keep her lunch down.

She wasn't sure what she had seen in his expression. One thing that she was certain of was that she was surprised to see him. She had known he would be her partner, but not how great he would still look. Nor had she realized how much he looked like her dead husband. Paul had been built like Jack, broad shouldered and strong. Kelly missed Paul deeply, even if she was never convinced that she had loved him. When she saw Jack she felt even guiltier, as if nothing had been real without him.

How could she feel that her life had been a waste without Jack? Paul had been good to her. He had died protecting her. He had been home every night at five and at work on time every morning. She never had to pick his socks off the floor. Paul always said, "I love you," before leaving the house or going to sleep. There really had been nothing wrong with her husband. He had been a good man.

Paul even put the toilet seat down, she remembered with a sigh. After his death, she had persuaded herself that she loved him. Kelly had managed to paint her marriage in rose colors. And it almost worked. She had thought that she had loved Paul, right up till this morning.

Then Kelly had seen Jack. She saw the muscles rippling under his immaculately cut sports jacket. At 6 feet, he was tall enough to make her neck ache when she looked up into his intense blue eyes. The strong line of his jaw and regal angles of his cheeks made her heart beat a little faster. No one deserved to look that good.

She was baffled by her emotions. The desire to swoon in front of him threw her off balance. The last three years had been really difficult. First, Paul's murder, then struggling with the decision to leave her lucrative paralegal position to become a detective. Kelly had always kept in shape, but the physical demands of police training were almost more than she could handle.

Add to that the trepidation she felt when handling a gun and, finally, the intensity of the graduation ceremonies. Now she was assigned to the Boulder Police department with Jack Hall for a partner. She really had not expected to still be attracted to him on such a physical level.

She knew it had been wishful thinking that she could bury the dreams of him and the intense emotions from that night long ago. The ten years felt like just yesterday. For a moment she lost herself in a flight of fancy, wishing she could return to that warm night years ago.

Jack was captain of the football team, she the captain of the cheerleaders. They were the perfect couple. He was a few inches shy of his full height, but still much taller than she. They ate lunch together to talk about football game logistics. They saw each other after practice for more discussions, walking on the sidelines of the field while they planned. With practices at the same time, and many other shared classes, everyone assumed they would get together. It was their destiny to go to the prom together.

The night of the prom had been perfect. The soft, warm night air encouraged a walk in the light of the full moon. After the prom he had taken her to a little known hiking trail near Boulder High School. Ten minutes of hiking later they came to a large old oak tree. Without warning, he swooped her up into his arms. They both laughed.

He held her close a moment before carrying her to the soft covering of grass under the tree. Tenderly, he set her down, on her back. While looking in her eyes he had slowly taken off his black tuxedo jacket. He had been so calm and sure of himself. His touch was gentle, peaceful, and exciting. He slowly unbuttoned his shirt, but didn't remove it. His strong chest and stomach muscles rippled in the moonlight. He looked better than perfect. Loosening the top button of his pants he had laid down beside her. She gently reached up and stroked his chest. Jack took her fingers and kissed them one at a time. He leaned over, pressing that wonderful hard body to hers and kissed her mouth. His tongue teased her lips until she opened them for him to explore her mouth. It had been her first real kiss. It was a perfect kiss.

Her heart raced even now thinking about his touch and his mouth on hers. Two fingers drifted up to her mouth and she felt her nipples tighten under her thin blouse as she allowed herself to remember his embraces from so long ago. It was crazy, but she wanted his touch again. She wanted to finish what they had started that night, and live happily ever after.

Kelly dreaded finding out he was married, or even worse, blissfully married. What was she thinking? Kelly had to start paying attention to her job. Bad enough Jack had seen her lose control and contaminate the crime scene, with bile nonetheless. He couldn't see her daydreaming on the job. She had graduated top of her class last month and now intended to show everyone that she could do what other detectives couldn't. Taking a deep breath, Kelly determined to get her mind back in the game, stop a murderer, and keep him locked up for good.

The hunting man found his prey again. Her shoulders squared, her head held high, she walked with a purposeful

stride. He could imagine the set of her jaw and the deter-
mination in her face as she made her way to the houses
across the street.

He itched to trace the line of her jaw with his finger.
Closing his eyes...lids sinking over blue, bloodshot eyes...
he brought up the image of her perfect face. Her eyes look-
ing into his with admiration, with acceptance, with prom-
ises of understanding. The image jumped and the face was
yelling, screaming, with madness in the eyes that peered
at him. The eyes disappeared into blood soaked holes as
his own lids snapped open. A word of denial on his lips
died amidst the inhuman giggle that rose from his throat.

Bringing his eye back into focus, through the scope was
hard, but doable.

He watched, hoping for an opportunity.

Kelly thought it was time to get some answers to impress
Jack and make up for her little scene this morning. She left
the crowd gathered around the police tape and walked across
the firm grass at the edge of the park. Looking both ways,
she carefully crossed the street to the first house on the block.
She could still see the yellow police tape as she walked up
the sidewalk leading to the house.

With determined steps, Kelly approached the house. It
was a somber-looking house, painted grey, with darker grey
trim. There even were fake white shutters fastened back
against the house by each of the windows. Kelly glanced
around at the neighbors' houses. They were all similar ranch
style homes. Most had porches, with a few steps like the ones
she now climbed.

Pausing at the top of the stairs, she looked back over her shoulder. The park was clearly visible. Anyone standing on the porch would have seen a commotion. The crime scene was near enough the residents should have heard the gunshots; might have even heard screams for help.

If they had heard the pleas, why hadn't they come to the women's aid? Were they just too scared? Kelly would understand if they had been. She might never forgive herself for her husband's death, but she could easily understand why others might be too scared to help strangers.

Kelly was annoyed when she saw Jack walking across the street with his long, ground-eating strides. He joined her on the porch just as she rang the bell. A little old woman with grey hair came to the door. Jack remained silent so Kelly started the interview

"Hello, Ma'am, I am Detective Kelly Swift," she began, flashing her badge. "This is my partner Detective Jack Hall. I am sorry to bother you at this early hour, but there has been a problem in the park across the street." To emphasize her words, Kelly motioned across the street.

The elderly woman shuddered as she saw the police tape and response vehicles parked there. Stepping square in front of the woman again, Kelly continued, "We are wondering if you heard anything strange last night? Or if you saw anyone you didn't recognize out and about?"

"No," the woman responded. She paused, seeming to think for a few moments before adding "No, I don't believe I did. What's wrong, officers?"

"I am sorry to say there has been a double homicide in the park. There were at least two shots fired so we hoped that someone on this block had heard something."

The lady's hands went to her mouth. "How horrible!" she gasped. "This is awful. And in my neighborhood, too!"

"Did you hear anything?"

"I am so sorry I can't help you," The elderly lady seemed honestly distraught. "My hearing isn't what it used to be, you know?" She rung her hands and bowed her grey haired head, "Oh, my, I just don't know what this town is coming to."

There really wasn't much else Kelly could ask her. Kelly took her name and phone number and left a business card in case she thought of anything else to report. Walking down the porch steps, Kelly reflected that the woman had obviously been horrified to hear about the murder. She had not known anything.

It was frustrating to Kelly that she wouldn't have even heard the shots, but then again she was probably asleep when it happened. Kelly couldn't think of anything intelligent to say to Jack, so she kept her mouth shut and what she hoped was a serious look on her face, as they walked to the next house on the block.

The unsettling man watched disgustedly as the male detective closed the distance to his woman. Would he ever get her alone? The scope was growing too heavy. It sagged in his hands. Infuriated, he jerked the scope back up to his eye and tried to focus once more. His eyes tired, he cursed the scope's lack of power. He wished he could see her features. What had she thought of the murder scene?

Had she understood his need, sensed his desire? Was his frustration evident? He was afraid the answer was, no. He would have to ask her, but for now he was just too tired. Longing to call out to her, to take her in his arms and ask forgiveness, he felt a tear blur his tired eyes.

He set down the scope. Feeling the dampness on his palms he scrubbed them on his slightly grubby blue jeans. Getting slowly to his feet, he felt his bones might break if he moved fast. Move too fast and his hold on the here and now might slip. When that happened he hurt people. He was always sorry, later, but that didn't help those he hurt.

Abrasively he took hold of his wayward thoughts. No, he was not responsible. It wasn't him that hurt those girls. Never him. It was...NO! He was tired. He wouldn't think about it...him. With a force of will he was unsure he had, he forced reality and the present back into focus.

Gingerly bending back over to retrieve the scope he put it in its case. He would retreat and get some rest, but the woman would be his. He would have his answers in time.

Slinging the scope strap over his shoulder he limped off. The woods swallowed him up as if he had never been.

At the next house, Jack listened as Kelly again asked the questions. The house was more brightly painted, and the couple younger, with two kids. The man had been just about to go to work, but politely paused to answer Kelly's questions. Unfortunately, the interview went much like the first, with the exception of the comments about diminished hearing.

After the third house with similar results to the first, Jack was getting restless. Kelly was very competent in her questioning of the residents. When she found out that two young men lived alone in the last residence, she had even thrown in a few questions that were not by the book. Maybe Kelly wouldn't be too difficult to work with. Jack was sure he could learn to think of her as just any old partner, eventually. Undoubtedly, he would stop looking at her butt. Someday. Maybe. Yes, she was showing she could be professional, and undoubtedly he would too.

Jack was confident his professional demeanor was steadily in place. At least he was until he turned to follow her down the front steps. Her scent wafted up to him as he trailed behind like a lost puppy. Who was he kidding? It was hard enough to work with a woman, but to work with this woman would be impossible. Every time she bent over or even just walked in front of him all he could look at was her tight butt. She was still in great shape. Jack wondered idly what she did to keep her figure so supple and curvy. It certainly looked like her muscles were strong and firm. He would love to find out. What was he thinking! He shook his head trying to clear it and forget about this impossible lust that kept invading his thoughts.

Kelly was about to start up the street to the next house when Jack stopped her. "I don't think anyone is going to have anything for us. Let's meet back at my office. Write up the initial report and go to lunch."

"Sounds like a good plan," Kelly said. She didn't have an office yet, so Jack's would have to work.

Chapter Five

It was only a short drive to headquarters. Kelly turned up the tunes on her favorite radio station, mildly surprised it had not changed since she left for college. Strains of "Tainted Love" pounded out of the speakers. The beat helped to center her and push some of her worries to the back of her mind. The drive was over far too quickly. She had not had enough time to analyze any of her feelings. However, she was able to get them under control. So when she got out of the car she looked calm to any casual observer.

Kelly Swift walked into Jack Hall's office with more dignity than she had displayed when he first saw her that morning. "So, how do you want to do this?" she asked.

Jack wondered if she meant the two of them working together or solving the case, so he simply asked, "Do what?"

"Divide up the case," Kelly replied, wondering what he thought she meant.

"Well, why don't you go down to the coroner?" Jack suggested, "I will go try to light a fire under the forensics people." Jack matched his actions to his words. Pushing back his chair and standing up, he walked to the door.

Kelly noticed his clothes didn't have a wrinkle in them as he held the door for her. She turned right and walked down the plain corridor to the stairs. Jack followed her out, but turned left instead and headed toward the brightly lit room at the end of the hallway.

Someone put workplace posters at each landing. The first one said "Report sexual harassment." There were others, but Kelly didn't pause to read them. She was lost in her own thoughts. She thought she might go crazy if they didn't turn up a lead to follow soon.

Two floors down she pushed through the double red doors to see a young man at a desk. He stood when she entered and stepped out from around the desk, "Can I help you?"

Kelly was unsure if he was blocking her way or just being polite. She decided it might be some of both. After all she was new and didn't have her badge out. She decided to take the more formal route, showing her badge as she introduced herself, "Hi, I'm detective Kelly Swift."

"I'm Dr. Doug Brown," the young coroner held out a hand as he gave his name. They shook hands. His grip was firm, competent. Kelly immediately liked him. He had at least two good qualities; he was friendly and protective of his environment.

Kelly asked without preamble, "How long will it be before you know anything about the women who were murdered this morning?"

"Well, I can give you the preliminary report tomorrow morning, about what I found at the crime scene. It will be a couple of days before I have a full autopsy report," Dr. Brown offered.

"Can you just tell me what you found at the scene so I can get a clue as to which way to jump on this thing?"

"I guess I could do that, but the written report will be more accurate."

"That's okay, I can read that tomorrow morning also," Kelly encouraged him.

"Well, the women appear to have been shot in the head with a large caliber round. There seems to be residue and some burn marks to indicate a close up shooting, I'll have to send a residue sample to the lab to make sure. The bullet penetrated from the back of their heads and exited the front blowing out their teeth and most of their faces in the process."

"So this will make them harder to identify?" Kelly wanted to make sure she had understood him correctly.

"It will make it impossible to do quickly. Even if there is a missing persons report it would be hard for kin to make a positive ID unless the women had some kind of birthmark." Doug confirmed her suspicions.

"Do they have any distinguishing marks?" Kelly wanted to know.

"I haven't gotten that far yet. I have to write the preliminary report on the crime scene before I can take a look at the bodies," he admonished her. "I'll write the report first. After that I can look at the bodies more carefully and let you know what else I find. It might cloud my opinions of the crime scene otherwise. It will, of course, take a few days for tox screens to get back to us. I'll let you know as soon as I have more."

Kelly turned to go, thinking that this had been a waste of time. The coroner's parting words, "I hope you catch this guy," caught her just as the door closed into the morgue. She walked back up the steps, frustrated. I sure hope Jack has more luck than I did, Kelly thought.

"Why, if it isn't fearless Jack Hall," Susan greeted Jack as he walked into forensics.

"Hi, Sue, you got anything on the double homicide from this morning?" Jack wanted to know.

"What do you take me for, a miracle worker? I just got back from the scene two minutes ago and haven't even had time to take off my coat, and you want answers?" Susan wasn't really annoyed, but it was good to keep the pushy detectives off balance a bit. Jack was always so sure of himself. She liked to throw him a few curves now and then. Acting offended was just one way to keep him from running over her lab in his desire to lock up the bad guys. Besides he had to know she wouldn't have anything but impressions yet.

"I know, Sue," Jack held up two hands in a placating gesture. "I just want your first impressions. I really want to catch this guy quickly. You know this is a college town. I don't want everyone running around scared and wondering if it could happen again." Jack was impatient, but he didn't want to push her so hard she kicked him out of the office.

"Well, if that's all you want," Sue paused a moment to gather her thoughts, before continuing, "I can tell you that the two women seemed to have been tied up and shot in the park. There was lots of blood on the ground below their feet.

There was not much sign of a struggle. One of the women's wrists has ligature marks on it, like she had been hanging there a bit before she was killed, the other did not.

"Judging from the bodies' core temperatures and the coolness of the night I think the murder happened about 3 am. I should know more for you in a couple of days. I am going to run their finger prints and try to get you an ID as soon as I can, but you know that takes a while."

"Did you have a chance to sift through the leaves under the tree?" Jack pried for more information.

"Umm, let me think, no, I don't think we did, I mean we always do a half assed job of searching a crime scene. Especially when it involves the first double homicide Boulder has seen since we can remember," Susan's voice dripped sarcasm.

"Okay, I will take that as an, 'of course we did,' and leave now." Jack was ready to beat a hasty retreat before she could come up with any more wit to throw at him. He was never sure why Sue was so touchy.

Jack called over his should as he left the room, "Thanks, Sue, I owe you one."

Sue waited till he was out of ear shot before she let out a huge guffaw. Jack was always a little too professional and serious. Susan really loved to goad him, kind of like the brother she never had.

Jack was so distracted, as he hurried down the hall he practically bumped into Kelly just before his office door.

"Ready for lunch?" Kelly asked before he could say anything.

"Sure," eating would offer him a chance to get his thoughts together. He was sure all he needed was a little time to be able to put all the loose pieces together. Actually he hoped that he could figure out what it was that bothered him so much about this case. Something was bothering him. He really hated it when he added two plus two and got 5.

"I know this little café right down on Pearl Street where we could eat." Jack offered.

"Sounds great," Kelly agreed. She smiled as he opened the front door of the police station and let her go first. He was always such a gentleman, even when he was younger. It was annoying that he treated her like a woman instead of a partner, but at the same time it was really nice.

He slowed his strides to match her shorter ones as they strolled down the Pearl Street Pedestrian Mall together. If it hadn't been for the serious look on their faces and the quickness of their step, they could have been any young athletic couple out during their noon break for a walk.

The Brown Cow served gourmet burgers and health food. They had a varied menu, but sprouts showed prominently in it. The restaurant was tucked into a small brown building shaped like a barn. There were framed posters of cows on many of the walls. The wall space that could be seen was covered with light pink paint and large asymmetric spots. Kelly supposed it was designed to look like a cow's spots.

When they walked up, Kelly groaned a little under her breath. The length of the line outside was substantial. "Want to go somewhere else?" she asked Jack.

"I think most of the people are getting it to go. It never seems to take very long." Jack obviously wanted to wait it out so Kelly patiently stepped into line.

Jack was right, the line moved quickly. They found a table in the back corner of the Brown Cow. They didn't even have time to strike up a conversation before the waitress was there.

"Hi, I'm Juliet and I will be your server today," said a young college student with blond hair. "What can I get you?" she asked as she set down two glasses of water.

"I would like the cheeseburger meal with French fries and a chocolate shake," Kelly said.

Jack gave her a funny look and said, "I would like the chef salad, extra sprouts and an iced tea please."

Juliet hurried off to turn in their orders.

"So, how did you wind up working in homicide, and as a detective no less?" Jack asked her.

"Well, it really is a long story. Let's just say I had to make a sudden career change when I lost my husband three years ago." Kelly avoided the question.

Lost! Yes, that meant she was single! Jack was careful not to let his relief show on his face. Relief? What, was he crazy? He could never get involved with her. He worked with her. She was his partner for goodness sakes. He would not do that again, get involved with a partner. He could never hope to feel her silky hair run through his fingers or to taste her sweet lips. It made him sad to think she was so close but so unattainable.

"Sorry to hear that." He responded. To change the subject he asked, "What did you learn from the coroner?"

"Nothing much. The girls appeared to be shot after they were hung up in the tree. One of them was tied up longer than the other one. No signs of struggle. So in short, it is a real mystery. No one heard anything." Some of Kelly's frustration leaked out, "The girls seem to have just let themselves be tied up and shot by a man who had a silent gun, and left no trace of himself. I really don't have a good feeling about this case. The coroner also said it would be hard to figure out who they were due to the mess the shot made of their faces. What did you find out?"

"About the same, but I have an estimated time of death at about 3 AM which would explain why no one saw the attack happen. Even in Boulder it's pretty quiet that early in the morning." Jack responded.

Their food came right. They were silent with their own thoughts while they ate. Jack noticed that while Kelly didn't exactly eat with gusto, she did steadily consume all of the food in front of her. She offered him some French fries, but he declined. He really had a hard time understanding where she put all that food or why anyone would put that kind of food in her body.

Juliet appeared with their bill and stood there expectantly. "I'll take that," Jack said, reaching out for the bill. After the waitress left he added, "I can expense it; you're probably not in the system yet." He went on, "Why don't we take my car back up the hill to the park and see if we missed anything this morning? Forensics should be done and we can dig around all we want."

"That sounds like a good idea. The murderer must have left some trace behind and we just didn't find it yet." Kelly said, trying to convince herself as much as Jack.

As they left the Brown Cow, Jack was sure to hold the door for her again. He liked to watch her go out first so he could see her bottom. Jack was still wondering how Kelly could keep her figure on a diet of milkshakes and fries.

They walked back to the station and he led her to the parking garage. She was surprised when he walked toward a beat up old Civic, but he walked past it to the black BMW parked two spaces over. Of course, a perfect car to fit a perfect man, Kelly thought. He could have stepped out of a fashion magazine, with his Calvin Klein style pants, his Polo shirt, and straight white smile. He even held the door open for her to get in first. The leather seats and wood inlaid interior were very posh.

As he climbed into the driver's seat he smiled over at her. The smile was friendly, but not suggestive at all. He was confident and knew he was handsome, or so it seemed to Kelly. His family had money, she remembered. That would explain the nice clothes and car; not the detective's salary that he made. She wondered what his house looked like. Ah, well, she would probably never find out. She was sure the house would be large enough for a big family, which he probably had by now. Jack was a fine catch for any woman. It made Kelly sorry she had left after high school. If things had been different she would have stayed. Her scholarship in English had not been at CU. Her parents had not been able to afford to send her to such an expensive university when she could go to Washington State University for free.

Jack drove the speed limit, not showing off the impressive handling of his car. She was sure he didn't always drive this slowly, but she didn't complain. Sitting in his car, intoxicated by the Cool Water cologne wafting off his skin, she floated in her own head until they pulled up at the crime scene. She made sure to open her own door and get out before he had time to come around. Chivalry was nice, but Kelly wanted Jack to learn that she could pull her own weight.

It felt natural to walk side by side. It was all Kelly could do not to take his hand as she would have in high school. His nearness set her nerves on fire. Parts of her couldn't concentrate on the task at hand. She wanted to throw him to the ground and kiss him right there, just as he had set her on the ground all those years ago. As soon as they approached the crime scene tape Kelly's thoughts were snapped back to the present. There was one lonely officer standing guard duty. They waved hi, and Jack said, "We just want to take another look around." Showing their badges, they ducked under the tape. Kelly made a show of holding the tape for Jack this time.

"Let's start at the edge of the tree's canopy and search outward in a circle," Jack suggested pointed at the tree the women had been found in. The soil under the tree had been scrapped down to the bare dirt. The fine rake marks in the ground looked like some Japanese garden. Smooth patterns ran around the tree base, radiating outward in concentric lines. Small rocks had been casually dropped here and there after being examined by the forensics crew. There was not even any sign of blood on the ground.

"You go counter clockwise and I will go clockwise. Our search can be a spiral so we overlap and don't miss anything." Jack hated having to spell out the way he liked to work. His old partner would have known what to do instantly, but his old partner seemed to know every inch of him and he did mean in a biblical sense of the word. He couldn't afford to let that happen again.

As Kelly ranged out from the tree she thought she saw something glint in the pine needles covering the forest floor just about 50 feet from the murder scene. She got down on her hands and knees and squirmed under the tree, chipping two nails and getting dirt under the other three on her right hand. She could feel the branches catching in her hair, tugging it out of shape. Ah, well, all in a day's work she thought.

Sitting back on her heels, doubled over, she extracted a pair of gloves from her pocket and slipped them on. She reached out to pick up the metal object and found it was stuck in the ground. She dug it out. As she looked at the sharp object pondering what it could be and if it was important Jack showed up beside her.

"What did you find?" he asked.

"I was just trying to figure that out,"

"Can I take a look?" he asked holding out his gloved hand. When did he have time to put on gloves? Kelly placed it in his palm and they climbed out from under the tree. Kelly couldn't help but notice that, after a quick little shake to dislodge a clinging pine needle, Jack Hall looked like he had that morning. He still looked fresh and clean and so very good. Kelly was very frustrated, both at the thoughts that kept creeping into her head and at her own state of dishevelment.

"Can I please have it back now?" she asked, a bit more snippily than she meant to. She was frustrated with her own errant feelings, not with Jack. She took a breath and determined to remain professional for the rest of the day.

Jack handed the object back to her. She still had no idea what it was, but Jack had a guess, "I think it might be the awl from a Swiss army knife. You know the smaller blade that is used for a leather punch."

"Okay, I guess I am not that familiar with Swiss army knives." Kelly said handing it back to him. She fumbled the blade while handing it back. Reflexively, Kelly reached to catch it. A sharp pain bit through the glove and into her palm as her fingers clamped down on the falling blade. A kind of light-headedness tingled up her arm till it hit her head. Her body betrayed her like this any time she was hurt by an unexpected cut.

Kelly pulled her hand back quickly, exclaiming, "Ouch!" She tried to play it down but Jack insisted on having a look at the cut. He gently peeled off the glove. It really was a bad cut. The edges were already pulling back to show it would probably need stitches. It looked deep. "I think you should go get that looked at," he said.

"We don't have time; we have to find this guy. A trip to the clinic would have to be followed by an official report. I don't want to take the time to do that," Kelly insisted. She really didn't want to look like a wimp. It was true they didn't have time, but the idea of inconveniencing Jack on the first day outweighed any thoughts of getting the cut stitched. She could go to the clinic and get stitches at the end of the work day. She closed her hand into a fist and held it tight in an attempt to stop the bleeding.

"How about a compromise?" Jack asked. "We can go to my house, clean your cut, and come right back here to keep looking." He held up a hand to forestall her objections adding, "It is only a half mile from here, it will only take a moment."

The idea of getting Kelly alone in his house was delicious. He wondered for a minute if that was why he offered. Stubbornly, he pushed the thoughts aside. He was not going to get involved sexually with another partner.

As blood dripped out of her tight fist she had to agree it looked bad, "Okay, I guess we will have to take the time or I might contaminate the crime scene with my own blood."

They walked back the way they had come, ducking under the crime scene tape again. Kelly was slightly amused. Before she had become a detective crime scene tape had meant that she was not allowed to go in. Now it meant that she should go in. In fact, it meant that her expertise was welcome and encouraged. She reflected that she would be doing a lot of ducking under bright yellow plastic ribbon now. It was good that she was young and limber from all the yoga she did each morning.

Jack helped her into the car. The blood on her hands, dripping slowly from her closed fist made it difficult to put on her belt. Jack pulled the shoulder harness out and leaned over her to fasten it. The close contact was wonderful and excruciating. His firm chest muscles brushed against her breasts. The manly smell of his cologne sent her into heady feelings of safety. The brush of his soft shirt against the back of her knuckles where she tried to hold her hands out of the way made her take a deep sigh.

It was all hard for her to bear. She didn't want to feel anything for him anymore. High school was a long time ago. She took a deep breath and sighed it out. Jack checked the seat belt with a quick tug asking, "You all set?" He had a concerned look on his face. The sigh must have sounded like she was tired.

"Sure am, I was just taking a cleansing breath," Kelly re-assured him. When Jack looked baffled, she hurried to reas-sure him, "I practice yoga and in yoga you learn how to re-lease stress through your breath."

"Cool. Maybe you could teach me how to do that some-time. Does it work well?"

"It works really well. The breathing by itself isn't as re-warding or refreshing as an hour of yoga positions done with the breathing. Everyone should try it sometime in his life." Kelly refrained from adding that it wasn't helping much to calm the sexual tension in her body right this moment. At least her palm had quit hurting.

Jack had climbed into the driver's seat as they talked, "Does it still hurt?"

Kelly was confused for a moment, wondering if he was asking about the yoga, then she realized he meant the hand. "Not really, and the blood has stopped. Maybe we should skip the stop to get it cleaned up. It probably wasn't as bad as I thought," Kelly added.

Shifting the car into drive and pulling out from the curb Jack said, "No way. We can take the time to get this cleaned up right so it doesn't get infected. Our case isn't going any-where."

"Besides that's my house just up there," Jack reassured her pointing to the two story house with the dark grey win-dow trim.

When they pulled up at his house, she let him help her out so she wouldn't get blood on his door handle, but she was able to trigger the seat belt release with her pinkie that wasn't bloody. His house was a beautiful old Victorian, and she was impressed with the immaculate yard. He must hire someone to do his yard. The landscaping was clean, almost perfect. No one had time to keep his yard looking that good and hold down a fulltime job.

"Beautiful yard," Kelly said.

"Thanks, I spend a lot of time on it," Jack flashed a smile back at her.

Kelly couldn't believe it. He was the perfect man. In addition to his charm and good looks, he did his own yard work. She wouldn't be surprised to learn he could cook too. Kelly could pull a weed with the best of them, but she preferred to spend her spare time working puzzles. They kept her mind sharp.

Jack led her into the entry hall and took her coat, which had a drying blood stain on it, from her hand. "I'll get the blood out of your coat in the kitchen. You can wash your hand in the bathroom," Jack said, pointing toward a bathroom just around the corner from the entry.

Chapter Six

When Kelly walked into the bathroom she was not prepared for the way she looked. She stared in shock at her torn blouse and the tangle that was her hair. Even her nails were dirty and chipped. She uncurled her fingers to look at the cut.

Her hand looked painful with the bright red gash across half the palm. It started weeping as soon as she released the pressure by opening her palm flat. The cut stung horribly as she rinsed it out, but it didn't seem to be too dirty. Next she wrapped toilet paper tight around the cut. After that was taken care of she turned her attention to her disheveled state. She straightened her hair a bit and tried to rub some of the dirt off her blouse. When she decided there was not much more she could do without a long hot shower, she left to find Jack.

Jack was hanging up her jacket on a hanger when she walked into the kitchen. It looked like the blood stain was totally gone from the jacket. Perfect clothes, perfect body, perfect yard, and now perfect housekeeper, what more could this man throw at her?

"Let me look at that cut." Jack led her over to a chair at a bar in his kitchen. She took a seat and let him carefully unwrap the paper to expose the wound. "It looks deep, but you did a good job cleaning it out. Let me bandage it up for you and it will be as good as new."

Jack leaned past her, reaching into a drawer and pulling out a first aid kit. Carefully, he applied antibiotic cream to the wound. Next came a few strips of butterfly tape. "This will help keep it shut until you can get it stitched up," he explained as he worked.

He finished his treatment with a clean white wrap over a gauze pad. As he wrapped her hand Jack thought about how much he liked taking care of her. She was strong and capable and hadn't whined at all about the cut. All of that just made her even more attractive. The dignity she could display even when her clothes were torn and her hand bleeding was amazing. She had a pride about her that said she wasn't used to being babied. It just made him want to baby her all the more.

Their eyes met, blue on blue, and held for a long moment. Jack couldn't help himself; she just looked so perfect sitting there, rough and tumbled though she was. He leaned in and pressed his lips to hers. When he didn't get decked right away he let his kiss linger on her lips.

Kelly was shocked. Jack was kissing her. The fireworks were going off again. She forgot to breathe. The kiss deepened and she actually wrapped her arms around him, pulling him into her. Feeling the wonderful hard muscles in his chest press against her breasts and she rose to meet him. He deepened the kiss and she encouraged him, parting her lips a little. His hand found the back of her head. He gently twined his fingers into her hair, locking them together.

His tongue met hers and they played for what seemed a long time. She remembered to breathe again and he was pulling back. He made some excuse or another for his behavior. She really didn't hear much of what he had to say. She was lost in feelings. She reached for him, but he was moving out of range too fast. He didn't even see her hand.

What had he been thinking? How could he have done that? Well, it wouldn't happen again. He would explain right now what the problem was. Kelly was a smart woman. She would understand and not be hurt by it. After all she had already been married. There was no way she could still feel for Jack what he felt for her. It had been ten years ago after all. And it had only been one night, one glorious night, but still only one night.

Jack started pacing the kitchen, five steps then turn, five steps then turn back. There wasn't much room to pace in but he had to pace to think. Kelly started to say something, but he held up his hand to forestall her. "Please let me explain." he said. He paced some more getting his thoughts in order. Just when he thought she would surely think he was mad if he took a moment longer to say anything, he figured out how to say it.

"Please, just listen. Not too long ago I got involved with someone I was working with. She was actually my partner, the one I had just before you." Jack started anxiously. He paused to take a deep breath. Now that he had started he would see this through no matter what the consequences. He couldn't keep this big a secret from his new partner; it would jeopardize their working relationship. He knew telling her

would ruin any chance they had at renewing their social relationship.

Kelly wondered where this was going. Oh, boy, this was
a bomb shell. She was not sure she wanted to hear it, but she
settled back into her chair trying to keep a passive look on
her face.

Jack continued, "She was a great partner. We connected
on many levels professionally, but we did not love each
other. Our relationship was purely sexual. It lasted about 6
months, until one of the department heads figured out she
was sleeping with someone in the force. I am still not sure
how they figured it out, but they did.

She refused to give up her lover, me, so they canned her.
If she had reported me they would have fired both of us. As
it is, I am responsible for her losing her job. I tried to get her
to turn me in, hoping they might spare her job even when I
knew they probably wouldn't. When she said, "No," I offered to turn myself in, but she insisted that they would fire
both of us. I know she was right, but I am still responsible.

I didn't love her. There was no reason to continue the relationship after we were no longer partners. She moved out
of state shortly after the incident. This was only two months
ago, but even if it was five years ago I still wouldn't want a
relationship with someone I work with." He finished and
held his breath, stopping his pacing and looking her square
in the eye.

He was ready for her to pass judgment on him. He knew
she would have to tell the captain now and that he would
most likely be fired. At the very least she would have to ask
for a different partner. That would raise questions after the
recent issue with his last partner and he couldn't afford the

questions. He was unsure why he told her, but he thought she had a right to know. Maybe by telling her she would see he wasn't right for her and they could head this off before it went any farther. The longer she sat there looking at him the more concerned he grew.

Kelly just stared at him. Her thoughts whirled in her head. He kisses me and then dares to tell me he doesn't want a relationship? How am I supposed to react? My body wants him and I thought I felt his body want me. There were lots of things she could say, but she settled on the least committal thing she could say, "You are right of course, I forgot for a moment that we had to work together."

Jack paused for a moment like he expected her to say something. Really, what could she say? There was no excuse and nothing she could do to absolve his guilt. She settled for hopping off the stool and saying, "Guess we should be getting back to the office."

They walked to the front door. He handed her an extra coat from his closet and helped her into it saying, "I'll bring your coat to work tomorrow when it is dry."

"Thank you, that is thoughtful," she said. It was driving her crazy to have him standing so close to her. She just wanted to get some distance. Actually, that wasn't true, she wanted to pull him into her arms and kiss him again. The taste of his lips was addictive. She knew no matter how many times she tasted him she would never get enough. It was better to stop it here, before it went further than either of them was prepared for.

Instead of kissing him again, she walked out of the house and made her way to his car. He still held the door open for her, like a perfect gentleman. The only thing that had changed was the feel of the air. It was charged with tension. Something would have to change if they were going to work together.

They rode to the station in silence. Jack wondered what she would do with the information he had just given her. The silence built on the ride back to work until he couldn't stand the tension and he had to ask, "Are you going to turn me in?" The shocked look on her face was enough of an answer in itself.

She was surprised that he would even ask, "Turn you in? Why would I do that? You are my new partner. What is past is past. I don't see why it would have to be dredged up again."

"Thank you," was all Jack could think of in response to this amazing answer. Kelly gained one more step in his approval of her. Too bad they worked together. There were so many things he would like to do with her... to her. Just thinking about her body next to his was enough to drive him crazy. He felt his pants get a little tighter in the crotch. He wasn't sure why she still held this power over him. He didn't like it. Or rather he liked it way too much and knew it would frustrate him to no end unless he found a solution for his libido.

Jack forced his attention back to the business at hand, with some difficulty. "I'll run this broken blade up to forensics and you can go home for the night. I'll see you in the morning. In my office. At eight," Jack said by way of dismissal pulling into his favorite parking spot. Stepping out of the car Jack walked up the stairs toward the offices.

Kelly, in a stunned silence, slowly opened her own door. She thoughtfully walked to her car and got in. It was almost quitting time, but she had expected to talk things over in his office. However, it was obvious that the one kiss they had shared was enough to throw him off balance. It was just as well, she needed time to adjust to this new wrinkle in her life.

What was she going to do? She wanted him badly. She really did, but she also understood that he would never have her while they worked together. She wanted this job just as badly. She owed it to her husband. It was the least she could do after getting him killed.

The irritated man waited. He was getting tired of waiting, but he could still do it if he had to. Absently he rubbed his bad leg. He hated how it slowed him down. He hated being tired. His spotting scope lay idly in his lap, out of its case and ready to narrow in on his prey.

She would come again. She would have to come. He could wait. He rested his head against the tree behind him and drifted. For a while the chirping of birds and the rustle of branches gently washed over him. The calm sounds lulled him, reminding him of happier time. A time when he had less obligations.

He sat outside his childhood house, making mud pies. The thick wet goo ran through his fingers, no so much dripping as oozing onto the ground. The nice round circle that this produced made the perfect size patty for his small hands. He scooped up a patty and tossed it at the closest bush, just to his right. Smiled as it made a very satisfying squelching sound, spreading its wetness through the branches.

Her voice came, loud and clear from the house, demanding he clean up the mess. He shuddered, even now as a grown man. Suddenly the man's point of view shifted. He was jerked out of the scene to float above it. He watched as the boy got up and went toward the house. He screamed at the boy to stop. No... to go. The boy didn't listen. Nothing the watching man could say or do would stop the child. He retreated deeper into his mind, powerless to stop the scene from unfolding before his closed eyes. He knew that even if he opened them he would still see the boy. That innocent boy...

Chapter Seven

The next morning Kelly's phone rang before she was out of the house. "Hello, Detective Swift," she answered it.

"Detective, this is dispatch. There has been another homicide, and the captain would like you to go straight to Central Park. Detective Hall will meet you there. You know where the park is?" the dispatcher asked.

"Yes, I know where it is. I'll go right now," was Kelly's reply. She hung up the phone, grabbed her keys and headed for her car. She knew Central Park well. It was across from the library downtown. She used to stroll there with her mom when she was little. Later, when she was in grade school, it had been fun to play in the ankle deep creek that flowed through it. In high school, it had been a good place to talk with your boyfriend.

Kelly drove there at a moderate speed. When she arrived Jack Hall was already standing there with that intense stare of his. He was looking at two young women who could have been her sisters; they looked so much like her. Both of them were hanging in a tree.

At first, Kelly had the bizarre thought that someone had removed the bodies from the morgue, brought them here, and hung them up. Then she saw the blood pool below their feet and came to the horrific conclusion that these were two new bodies. Four dead bodies in two days! This was unbelievable. It was starting to look like they had a serial murderer on their hands.

Jack stared incredulously at the two new bodies hung from the tree. His priority had shifted from finding this guy to stopping this guy. It put a whole new set of priorities on the case. He had to find this guy. Fast! Jack still didn't have any idea what he was going to do when Kelly walked up.

"I'll go ask the neighbors if they saw anything," she volunteered right away.

"Right. I'll go do a walk about and check for clues, but it looks like the same M.O. as last time," Jack said. He didn't have much hope of finding anything that would help them. "Let's meet back here in about an hour, unless you find someone who will talk." Jack said in a kind of detached voice.

Kelly quickly strode off toward the houses across the street from the park. She didn't want to look at those women any longer than she had to. She would let Jack handle that part of the investigation. It wasn't a queasy stomach that made her feel this way. It was just that the two women looked so much like her. It was eerie.

The disturbing man snapped awake. What woke him? The last he remembered he was screaming in his head...

no, he wouldn't think about that. So what had woken him? His post was too far away for the noises from the ghastly scene to wake him. He wanted to be far enough away that they couldn't stumble on him by accident.

Then he saw the squirrel. It was nibbling the grass near his leg. The little creature's rear legs were on his leg, butt in the air, while its head was stretching toward the ground. The man's lips twitched up in a smile as he reached to gently brush the short brown fur with the back of his hand. Immediately, upon contact, the squirrel scampered off.

Free of this encumbrance, the man quickly raised the scope to his eye and peered from the concealment of the trees. The place was already swarming with police. They were struggling to deduce what he already knew. He could almost hear them asking "how could this be happening?"

The shady man smiled. He swept the park with his scope. He knew he would find her. She would want to pursue every possible lead in trying to catch the murderer. He knew she was there. He would find her. His nest was ready. He had a plan. She would be his this day.

None of the occupants of the houses yielded any answers to Kelly's questions. After asking at five different houses, she gave up and headed back to the crime scene. This time there was no crawling under trees, no little metal knife, and no cut hand. There was also no trip to Jack Hall's very nice house, and no hope of a kiss… or more.

"Anything?" Jack asked when Kelly strode up to him. She just shook her head dejectedly.

"Let's see if the lab has anything for us," Jack suggested.

"Okay, I'll meet you there," Kelly responded.

They both walked to their cars in silence, except for the single, "Thanks," that Kelly uttered to the police officer that held the crime scene tape as they ducked under it. The drive back to the station was short. They both arrived at the same time despite Jack being stopped by a red light that Kelly just managed to squeak through. She suspected he had broken a few traffic laws to catch back up.

They both got out of their cars at the same time and walked upstairs, side by side. Jack didn't pause at his office so Kelly followed him. He led the way to the forensics lab. By unspoken agreement, maybe because he was the senior partner, she let Jack ask the questions.

"Hey, Sue, did you find anything on that blade that I gave you?"

"Sure, Jack, I work miracles every day," Susan responded sarcastically.

"We had another double homicide this morning," Jack snapped back, "same M.O. as the last one."

This news seemed to deflate Susan. "Sorry, I didn't know," she demurred. "I'll let you know as soon as I have anything,"

"Thanks, Sue, I didn't mean to snap. I guess four dead women in 24 hours just gets to me," Jack allowed by way of apology on his way out the door.

The door had just swung shut behind them and they had taken two steps down the hall, when Susan rushed out. "Wait! I found something."

"This just came in off the blade you found at the first crime scene." Susan held up a sheet of paper. "The blade had a partial print, and the computer just got a hit on IAFIS. Don't ask me how it got a match so fast. I wasn't able to lift the print with dust." Susan was on a roll, seemingly forgetting the urgency of the case. "I had to put it in the chamber and used cyanoacrylate fumes to get the partial to show up. Next I took a picture and scanned the print into the FBI computer."

Susan took a deep breath, but Jack interrupted before she could continue, "Sue, what did you find?" he asked forcefully, pointing at the paper. This brought Susan up short.

She jolted, like a kid who had been caught being naughty by her parents. "Right, his name is Frank White. Best of all he has a record for abuse and battery of woman," she finished triumphantly. After a short pause, she seemed to realize what she had said and added, "Well, it really isn't good, except in the context of the case. I mean I really don't approve of someone battering women…"

Kelly hastened to reassure her, "We know what you mean," she said laying a hand on the woman's arm to get her to stop rambling.

Jack grabbed the note, "Looks like a current address" he observed. "Sue, you're the greatest!" he said, looking her in the eyes.

Jack turned and was out the door a second later. Kelly jogged to keep up as they passed Jack's office again and headed to the garage. When they reached the concrete of the garage floor Jack broke into a trot, not stopping until he reached his car. This time he didn't open the door for her. She actually beat him to the car and hopped in herself, calling out, "You drive."

Jack handed Kelly the note and Kelly read it out loud, "Frank White. 5307 Diagonal Highway East." Kelly paused, then added, "Where is that? I didn't know there was anything that far out on Diagonal Highway."

"That address is in the Gold Rush Apartment complex, on the Diagonal Highway, as you go toward Longmont, out of town." Jack informed her. "The apartments were built about a year after you left." Jack couldn't keep the last from sounding like an accusation.

He was still bitter at her for leaving right after that night. He had wanted to get married, to have kids, and have a life together. She had said she had to go, that she couldn't afford to stay. It still hurt, even though he knew she needed the scholarship.

"I have a plan," Jack continued without letting any of his resentment show. "That area doesn't offer much cover, but if we pull into the complex we may be able to park in front of another apartment so he doesn't see me coming."

Kelly was okay with the plan right up to the point when he said, '…see *me* coming.' She interrupted, not giving him a chance to finish his thought. "Whoa, hold on there. What do you mean, '*me*?'" she demanded.

"I mean, 'me', as in myself, as in singular, as in you keep in the car. I can't risk you messing something up. This is going to be tricky and I don't want to panic the guy." Jack couldn't imagine why she was making such a big deal out of this.

Kelly was seething now. She had put up with a lot over the last two days from her new *partner* and she had just about enough of this chauvinistic attitude from him. She decided to draw the line and dare him to step over it.

Through clenched teeth she continued, "Now you listen here. I have had enough of this stuff from you. Opening doors was nice and the gentlemanly thing to do. Then you bandage my hand and clean my coat. Then you kiss me. I won't even go there. You have been running this whole show like I'm some poor little intern who can't take care of herself. I have news for you! I. Am. Your. Partner. We work together," she said snapping out each word like it was a whip.

The man was surprised they would choose to come here. What had tipped them off to this place? He was more puzzled than scared, withdrawing into himself and into his hiding spot. Why were they here? What had they found? Carefully he let the door shut and suddenly he was a 7 year old boy crawling frantically into the coat closet in that house.

The boy hurt all over. Stiff and sore as only one of her lessons could make him. Shaking he sat behind the coats and prayed she wouldn't find him this time. Wished that if she did her temper would be gone and she would take him in her arms and tell him what a wonderful child he was. She could do that; he knew she could. Sometimes she even did.

But the man watching, through the boys eyes, knew that this was not one of those times. Desperately, almost violently, he tried to wrench himself from the scene. He failed. Helplessly he saw her hand part the clothes that hid him. Crouching with his hands in front of his face he felt her hand squeeze, vice like, around his arm. Without any warning, his perception snapped. Thankfully he floated above the scene and only had to watch it play out, not live it again. By the time the boy was cleaning up the blood in the bathroom the man was curled in a fetal position crying.

As the vision faded, he realized where he was again. He quickly stood, ran his hands down his front, smoothing his rumpled clothes. He took a deep breath to steady his shaking hands, and his resolve. He had to be ready when they came for him. There were two of them; not what he wanted.

He would have preferred to take the woman alone, but he could handle both of them. When this came to a head he would be ready for them!

Jack parked the car in a space near the apartment building they wanted. He paused behind the wheel. Sitting in stunned silence, Jack absorbed her words. Quietly, he said, "I was thinking that your hair, build and eyes make you look too much like the murder victims. Your looks alone might alert him to something being up. Whereas, with my suit, I can pass myself off as a salesman. At least until I have to identify myself." Having said this he reached into the back seat and pulled out a briefcase that she had not noticed before. He left Kelly sitting in stunned silence in the car.

Wow, I really blew that, she thought. How could I have been so hot headed? He wasn't just trying to protect me or run away with this case he was ... right. Even though it galled her to admit it, he was right. She would probably alert Frank to something being up just because of how she looked. Even if he didn't suspect cops, it might tip the scales of his sanity to see one of the girls he 'murdered' come walking up to his apartment and knock on the door.

In truth they had no idea how he would react. This made it a very dangerous situation in an apartment complex with thin walls. They already knew he had a criminal record, and that he had a gun. It wasn't a very far stretch that he could start shooting when Jack tried to arrest him. If he started shooting, lots of innocent people could be hurt. She had been an idiot. What was worse, she had let her mouth carry her away. She felt like a fool.

It was just after she admitted to herself what an idiot she had been that she saw Jack knock on the door numbered 22B. His mouth said something, but the window was up and she was too far away to make out the words. She imagined it was something like, "This is the Boulder Police. Open up." It could have just as easily been, "Hi, I am selling encyclopedias and I would love to leave you with a free sample."

After a short time he pounded on the door again. This time Kelly could hear it from inside the car. Jack seemed calm, but Kelly could read the set of his shoulders and see that one hand was clenched into a tight fist. It was the hand he had used to bang on the door. It was like it refused to go back to relaxed after attacking the door.

Jack's hand hurt from banging the side of his fist into the door. He shouted again for Frank to open up. This time the door opened a crack. Jack's nerves were on edge. Everything came into sharp focus. Frank stood in the doorway, peaking out through a crack that was just big enough for Jack to make out two shifty brown eyes below a receding hairline. Frank's belly protruded from his grubby white t-shirt, which had red stains on it. His dirty blue jeans were held up by a belt and only one rough, grubby hand, with dirt under the cracked nails, was visible.

"I ain't done nothing wrong and I ain't coming out," he said and slammed the door in Jack's face.

Going into hyper drive Jack brought his knee to his chest, aimed with his foot and kicked in the door. Frank was ready for him. Before Jack could stop him, Frank launched his not unsubstantial weight into Jack. They both tumbled backwards into the rail, saving them from a fatal drop off the stairs. Jack, taken by surprise, collapsed onto the landing.

The wind was knocked out of him, but he ignored it as he rolled to his feet. Frank was already half way down the stairs. Jack took in two large gasping breaths and took off after him. Jack couldn't believe that Frank could move that bulky body of his so fast, but he guessed that getting charged with murder could do that to a guy. By the time Jack got down the stairs Frank was almost to his car.

Jack was starting to be afraid he wouldn't be able to catch Frank, when suddenly Frank pulled up short. Kelly was standing just in front of Frank with her gun trained at him. He wasn't moving. By the time Jack got to Kelly's side, Frank was on the ground, face pressed into the concrete, with Kelly standing over him, gun drawn. It was enough to make Jack forgive the tongue lashing she had just given him.

Jack knelt down and handcuffed the prone man. "Not too smart," Jack whispered in Frank's ear as he jerked the man to his feet.

"You okay?" Kelly asked Jack.

"Yeah, just a few bruises. I guess I'll be needing a new pair of pants, too," he joked, looking down at the hole in the knee of his immaculately pressed pants. Kelly laughed a little, letting some of the tension flow out of her. Maybe he had forgiven or forgotten the harsh, impulsive speech she had made earlier.

They both had one eye on Frank. Neither of them wanted to give him an excuse to try something. Without warning Frank let out a string of abusive words that cumulated with, "little auburn haired wench, I will see you dead for this. I would have gotten away if you hadn't showed up."

This really set Jack off. He couldn't believe how protective he felt right now. Jack stepped between Kelly and Frank. He could feel the heat of his anger burning up his face. This piece of dirt had called his partner every name under the sun and threatened to kill her. Jack was about to beat the man into the ground when he heard the siren and saw the police car roll into the parking lot. Summoning all of his control, he shoved down on his rage. He took Frank by the shoulder and pushed him none too gently toward the black and white cruiser.

"Shut up and get into the car," Jack said while pushing him into the back of the patrol car. "Read him his Miranda rights," Jack snapped at the officer driving the car. He didn't trust himself to say more. Jack was so mad he didn't think he could string two sentences together much less get through the Miranda for this scum bag.

Jack knew that he could easily compromise the case right now. He didn't need this scum walking just because Jack couldn't control his temper. Jack shut the door firmly, intentionally not slamming it. He turned his back on Frank and walked back toward Kelly.

Nice of the back up to show-up he thought. Jack guessed that Kelly had called them in right after Jack had started for the apartment. The sirens and subsequent arrival of the patrol car had kept Jack from doing something that he would get in trouble for, even if he wouldn't regret it later.

Jack turned to Kelly and in a terse voice said, "Let's go see what this scum was hiding in his house."

Kelly kept quiet, recognizing the mood Jack was in. She was a little afraid of him in this mode. She knew he wasn't angry at her, or at least she hoped he wasn't angry with her. She had called for back-up without being told to. What else was she supposed to do when he took off to arrest a dangerous suspect without her? She told herself that she did the right thing. Her emotions were a mixture of pride and concern. Jack was acting strangely, which was reason for concern, but she had pulled a gun in the line of duty. She had kept her head, not had to use the gun, and made the arrest, which was a reason for pride.

They walked across the leaf-strewn parking lot in silence. Each wrapped in his own thoughts. Kelly had no idea what Jack was thinking and it worried her. She kept quiet anyway, knowing that he would tell her in his own time.

Jack was still shaking, even if it didn't show on the outside. If Frank had been carrying his gun. If Frank had been a little faster. If there had not been a railing. If. If. If. There were a lot of ifs and it scared Jack to let his thoughts go there. If any little thing had been different Kelly could have been hurt. If she had been hurt, he wasn't sure what he would do.

Man, he had it bad for her, but he was determined not to repeat his mistakes. He would not date her, sleep with her, or even kiss her again as long as she worked on the force with him. It was driving him crazy, so he poured all of those intense emotions into his stride walking across the parking lot.

When he reached the stairs he was several strides ahead of Kelly. He paused to let her catch up and his emotions calm down. She needed to know he wasn't upset with her, even if he didn't dare to tell her why he was upset. He would never be able to admit he loved her. If he ever told her, there would be no going back. It might even be worse than that. What if she rejected his love? Rebuked him? He had kissed her and pushed her away. He had just now shown what a hot head he could be. What if she was afraid of him and wanted nothing to do with him now or ever? He couldn't handle that kind of rejection, so he would never tell her how he felt.

Kelly caught up to Jack at the bottom of the stairs. He seemed to pause and take a breath. When he released the breath in a huge sigh, he seemed to be back to his old self. Kelly wondered what had been going on in his mind. She was scared to ask, bowled over by her own feelings right now. Feelings of relief they had caught Frank and feelings of anxiety over Jack's state of mind. She was also repressing the feelings that threatened to overwhelm her. Feelings surfacing from her husband's tragic death.

More than anything she wanted to pull Jack into her embrace and hold him, and be held by him, for a few hours. The intensity of this desire overwhelmed her for a moment and she paused beside him. She knew that if he so much as started to reach for her she would be lost. Her heart already belonged to him, though there was no way she would ever be able to tell him that. He had made it clear that he didn't want her in the same way she wanted him, at least not while they worked together. There was no way she could give up being a detective. It was her cross to bear, her atonement.

Besides, if he learned what had happened with her husband he would never want to talk to her again, much less look at her.

Jack finally dared to speak, "You did a great job back there. Thanks for saving my butt."

Kelly could only think of one thing to say, "You're welcome, that's what partners are for."

They walked up the stairs in silence, but this time it was less strained. Kelly was relieved Jack hadn't been angry with her. She had played by the book and it seemed it was the right thing to do. He obviously had something else on his mind. Probably something that had nothing to do with her. Kelly sighed her own little sigh, not loud enough for Jack to hear, but enough to help her center and calm her thoughts. She followed Jack into the apartment.

Stepping into the apartment was like stepping into despair. The smell was overwhelming. There were dirty clothes strewn over the floor. The bed was in the far corner, but the sheets looked like they had not been washed in a year. The chair in the corner didn't have any feet so it sat with its bottom flush with the floor. The carpet was an indistinguishable grey color, but may have been off white at one point in time. There was some kind of country western music playing in the background. It seemed to be coming from the kitchen. Kelly almost gagged when she saw the dirty dishes strewn over the counters. Open bottles of whiskey and vodka filled the little remaining surface area. How did Frank stand the filth that surrounded him in this apartment?

Jack was searching the only other room in the small apartment. It seemed to be a TV room, but had clearly been intended for a bedroom when they built the apartment. Kelly joined him in the 'bedroom.'

"Looks like he was in here when I knocked on the door," Jack said.

The large screen TV was playing "Paint Your Wagon," an old time western musical. That explained the music in the background. A table sat in front of the TV. A rusty folding chair sat facing the table and the TV. On the table were some newspaper articles about animal abuse cases. And there was the broken pocket knife sitting on the table. Jack and Kelly were both careful not to touch anything in any of the rooms. When Jack saw the knife, he set his jaw and a look of determination came over his face.

"Come on, we had better get out of here before forensics gets here. Don't touch anything, not even the door knobs," Jack said as he started for the front door. Kelly followed him out and down the stairs, reaching the parking lot just as Susan and her team pulled up and piled out.

Jack pointed at the busted in door saying, "Make sure you bag the pocket knife you find in the bedroom. Oh, and you might want nose plugs. It is pretty ripe in there."

Jack turned to Kelly, "Let's go back to the station to see what this scum bag has to say for himself."

Chapter Eight

Jack made sure not to open Kelly's door for her this time. He was confused about why she had been so upset with him just before the arrest. Heck, he was just confused. His mind was deep into solving the case, making sure all his bases were covered. He knew they had to get Frank to confess.

The evidence was circumspect at best. Jack was sure that Frank was guilty, but it would be hard to prove in court, unless the blood on his shirt proved to be the victims'. Somehow, Jack thought that would not be the case; it wasn't ever that easy. Frank had been meticulous, and except for the broken blade, they might not have caught him at all.

Jack was hardly aware of the turns he made getting back to the station. He drove on autopilot. Besides the case he was totally in turmoil over his emotions for Kelly. Even when they were both teenagers the sex had been unbelievable. They had truly been in love, and Jack was sure it wasn't just the puppy love variety. Why couldn't they have done as their hearts commanded, not their heads? If they had eloped instead of doing the 'smart thing' how different would life be now?

Jack let his mind drift even further into the fantasy that would have been his life. Kelly could have had a part time job doing something she loved. They could have shared his house or one a little bigger with their three kids and two dogs. He smiled a little at the image of the kids and dogs roughhousing with him in the big back yard. His idyllic daydreaming was interrupted by Kelly yelling, "Look out!"

Jack's full attention snapped back to the road just in time to miss the pedestrian that had stepped unexpectedly off the curb. His heart raced and it took a moment for him to recover from the scare. His first instinct was to snap out, 'I saw him,' but he thought better of that as soon as the fright wore off and just said, "Thanks, that would have ruined his day."

Kelly laughed a little at his poor joke. She had been lost in her own thoughts and had almost not seen the person on foot either. When she saw him she had yelled without thinking. A good thing she did, too, because it sounded like Jack hadn't seen the guy at all. "So just what were you thinking about so hard?" Kelly inquired.

No way was Jack going to mention the ideal family he had pictured. He settled for a safer and somewhat true answer, "I was thinking about Frank's interrogation."

"They taught us a standard list of questions to use in a murder investigation. Don't you use those same questions?" Kelly asked.

"In a standard investigation it is always good to open with those questions and improvise from there. However, you may have noticed this is not a standard investigation." Jack reflected that he probably would open with the standard questions anyway, but he was feeling defensive.

"Okay, I get it," Kelly replied curtly.

Kelly sat back and crossed her arms over her chest sending clear signals that she was not approachable. Of course, if she had thought about it she would have known that the standard questions were only a crutch for new detectives. A more seasoned detective might have developed his own line of questions to work from. She should have thought before she spoke. Again.

The rest of the car ride was in silence. Kelly kept sneaking looks at Jack out of the corner of her eye. He had a strong, handsome profile. Just enough fullness to his lips, a strong chin, and enough neck, so that she could bury her face in it. She would love to nuzzle up to him. Maybe if she just got a kiss in on that neck he would relent and be nice to her again. She remembered that he loved that. Kelly was trying to find a way to justify trying when they pulled into the station garage.

She was torn. It was for the best that her thoughts were interrupted, but she still really wanted to just cuddle up to him and try to make him forget his annoyance with her. When the car came to a complete stop she hopped out and started for the stairs, not waiting for Jack.

Jack got out of the car more slowly, grabbing the IAFIS report and locking up. Kelly had leapt from the car like she couldn't wait to get away from him. Perhaps he had been acting a bit snobbish he reflected. Almost hitting the pedestrian had rattled him; it wasn't like him to let his attention wander. Finding Kelly at the crime scene yesterday morning had really thrown him off. Even if she hadn't been there, he would have been shaken at seeing a double homicide in his town. Now, two. Add to that the fact they resembled his first sweetheart and his week would have already been off to a bad start, Kelly or no Kelly.

Put all those into two days: an old lover, a new partner, and gruesome murder scenes. Jack was surprised he wasn't having a nervous breakdown. He laughed under his breath at the image of himself huddled in a corner sucking his thumb. "Never," he said out loud even though he was all alone. He pushed his thoughts aside and exited the car.

Kelly waited for Jack to catch up outside his office, taking the few moments to relax and calm herself. She didn't want to screw up and snap at Jack again.

"Shall we head to the interrogation room?" Jack asked as he approached.

"Sure," Kelly's quickly responded. Apparently they weren't going to discuss their approach first. Was she 'good cop', or 'bad cop?' She would let Jack run the show a bit longer. That was fine by Kelly, for now, but only as long as it took for her to learn the ropes. Jack would learn she was an equal part of the team.

Jack and Kelly waited outside the interrogation room for Frank to be brought in. "Do you want to go in with me, or observe from here?" Jack asked Kelly.

"I can handle anything he chooses to throw at me." Kelly tried to sound determined. "I'll go in, thanks."

Jack held the door for her as they stepped into the interrogation room. Frank sat before them with a belligerent look on his face.

Before either Jack or Kelly could say anything Frank spat out, "You have no right to keep me here! No right to bust down my door."

"How about resisting arrest for a start," Jack said in a calm voice.

"I didn't resist 'til you broke my door," Frank insisted. "How am I supposed to explain that to the manager? I stopped when your partner flashed her badge at me."

"We are not here to argue the finer points of the law with you. We are here to talk to you about the four women you murdered." Jack kept quiet after that, watching Frank's reaction.

Frank started to protest, got out two words and stopped. Kelly thought he truly looked surprised at Jack's accusation. Finally, Frank asked, "What women?" Not the most exonerating thing he could have said.

"Just when were you last in Chautauqua Park" Jack demanded.

"How do you know I was ever there?" Frank asked suspiciously.

"Just answer the question." Jack sounded calm and patient, like he had all day. Kelly suspected he didn't feel like that at all.

"Okay. About a week ago, I guess." Frank stopped to think before he continued, "Yeah, it was a week ago. I went for a walk. I remember because..." he looked at Kelly and reddened. "Because I almost lost my pants. My belt broke so I stopped to fix it."

"Is that so?" Jack didn't begin to believe Frank's lies.

"Yes. Yes it is. I took off the belt, sat down and tried to punch a new hole in it. Darn knife broke, so I just held up my pants until I got back to my car," Frank said.

"You see Frank, we have a way of telling when you are telling the truth and when you aren't. I can tell you are making this up, or rather that you already had the fabrication ready in case we found something to link you to the case." Jack seemed very sure of himself. Kelly wasn't so convinced. She thought Frank might be telling the truth.

Jack was going on with the questioning, so Kelly shelved that thought and listened to the interrogation. "That is convenient since we found your knife under a tree there. The problem is I think you just lied to me. I think you broke your knife when you tied up the women you killed."

"I didn't kill no one! Why won't you believe me?"

"Because you haven't given me a good reason to believe you. The women you murdered all had auburn hair, like my partner. You threatened her when she arrested you. She was just doing her duty, but you said you would kill her. I assume you remember that?"

"I...I was drunk. Too much to drink last night. I wasn't in my right mind." Frank protested. He was starting to sound desperate. Kelly really didn't think he looked like a murderer. Frank's eyes pleaded with her to believe him.

"You were drunk or insane? Kind of the way you must have been feeling last night when you killed those poor women?" Jack was pushing as hard as he could, but Frank just wouldn't crack.

"I have no idea what you are talking about! I was drinking all night," Frank insisted, "with my friend."

"Sure you were. What is this friends' name? How do I get a hold of him?" Jack asked.

"His name's Johnny. He lives in the same apartments I do. He ain't got no telephone number and I don't want you to surprise him like you did me," Frank shot back.

The possibility of an alibi just made Kelly even more unsure. She really had a hunch they had the wrong guy. She needed to make sure before more women wound up dead. She decided to risk Jack's ire with a question of her own.

"Frank," Kelly began gently, "if this friend of yours can vouch you were not at the park when the women were murdered, that means we can't prove you did it. You need to give us his last name and an apartment number so we can verify your story," Kelly urged.

"Yeah, okay, okay, I see your point. Colin, Johnny Colin is his name. He lives just below me in 12B. You go ask him. He'll tell you I don't know nothing about no murders."

Jack snapped, "Trust me, we will, buddy." He strode to the door and opened it. Looking at the officer standing in the doorway Jack said, "Take this scum away and lock him up."

Kelly followed Jack out of the room and to his office.

As soon as Jack shut the office door he demanded, "Well, what did you think?"

Kelly considered carefully. She had thought he was guilty when they left the apartment complex. He had the knife that they could link to the scene of the first crime by the broken blade they found. He said he would kill her and referred to the way she looked, but after the interview she just wasn't sure.

He might have been mad at her because she stopped him from getting away. He had probably been upset about her drawing a gun on him. He obviously was predisposed to hate women in authority. However, he claimed to have an alibi and something kept tickling the back of her brain, something she couldn't quite put a finger on.

Carefully Kelly responded, "I think we should go check out this alibi of his before we make up our minds completely."

"I suppose you are right," Jack allowed out loud. Privately he had no doubts at all. They had caught the scum ball. He was as guilty as they came. He had threatened to kill Kelly. He all but said it was because she had auburn hair. He obviously hated women who were self-assured. The women who were murdered wore the clothes of successful business women. He had an alibi that would probably be full of holes. Jack had to admire Kelly for being willing to keep an open mind until all the facts were in, even if his 9 years of experience thought she was being naive.

"Let's go check out this Johnny Colin," Jack said as he stood up from his desk and strode across the room to open the door for her. When they reached the car he opened her door first again. The fact that he was back to being a gentleman was not lost on Kelly.

On the drive back across town she thought about the changes in Jack. Maybe he had just needed her to stand up to him. Maybe he could treat her as a professional. Is that what she really wanted? Of course it was, wasn't it? Maybe he really did think that kiss had been a mistake. Or what if he hadn't felt for her what she had felt for him with that kiss. That had to be it. He no longer felt the fireworks when they kissed. That thought made Kelly sad, though she knew it could never work between them.

With all the police cars gone from the parking lot, the apartment complex looked calm again. No one would have ever known they had arrested a murderer there this morning. The busted in front door had been set back in place. There were no broken windows or bullet holes in the building. That was it! Kelly finally had one thing that had bothered her.

Kelly said, "Where was Frank's gun? I mean he didn't pull it on you and it wasn't found at his house. So where was it?"

"He probably dumped it," Jack said.

"I suppose he could have, but why keep it after the first murder, only to dump it after the second? Sudden change of heart?"

Jack didn't even seem to think about it, "Maybe he was having second thoughts, or maybe he lost it after the second set of murders. I'm not sure, but that guy is guilty; all we have to do is prove it."

By the time they got to Johnny Colin's apartment it was early evening. It had been a busy day and Kelly knew she would be more than ready for dinner, but the interview came first. Before they even walked all the way across the parking lot they saw Johnny's apartment door open. A middle-aged, pot-bellied man walked out. He had on a clean shirt, but his pants looked a little lived in. As Jack approached him, Jack caught a whiff of body odor that suggested the slovenly Johnny hadn't showered since his last binge.

"Johnny Colin? I am Detective Hall and this is my partner Detective Swift. We have a few questions for you," Jack said blocking Johnny's path.

"I'm on my way to the bar," Johnny responded. Ogling Kelly, he added, "but you could come with me if you wanted."

"That won't be happening," Kelly deadpanned. "Now will you answer our questions here or at the police station?"

"Okay, don't get in a tizzy. I'll answer your questions."

Jack started again, "Do you know Frank, your upstairs neighbor?" At Johnny's nod he continued, "Do you know where he was last night?"

"Yeah, we went to The Dive to have drinks, if you know what I mean," he winked at Kelly.

"How late did you stay at The Dive?" Jack continued.

"We were going to be there until they closed. Who knows, maybe we made it, maybe we didn't. I think I remember Frank getting a bloody nose. We had to leave when his nose started spurting. They got real upset about the mess. Is Frank in some kind of trouble?"

"Please, just answer the questions, Mr. Colin," Jack stated. "Why would he have a bloody nose?"

"He hit on some topless dancer. Hell, he didn't just hit on her. He tried to take her home; got his hands all over her boobs and she took offense and smashed his nose with her fist. Next the bouncer came, I think, and hit him again. I mean that's extreme. If they didn't want to be touched they wouldn't dance there, would they?"

Jack looked over at Kelly. She actually seemed to be turning red. Jack was getting pretty ticked off too. He thought he had better get this wrapped up fast before he took a swing at the guy.

"Where did you go after they closed?"

"Damned if I know. I was so trashed I couldn't see straight. I guess we came back here. I mean I woke up in my apartment." Johnny took one look at Jack and decided he had better add, "I mean it is okay we were plastered. We didn't drive or anything. The Dive is only two blocks away. We walked."

"I am aware of where The Dive is located." Jack said, bringing him up short. "So, you don't know what time you got home or if Frank went home?"

"Yeah, that about sums it up, now can you tell me what is going on with Frank?" Johnny asked.

"We'll get back to you on that." Jack dismissed him, "That is all the questions we have for you right now."

Johnny shrugged his shoulders and continued walking toward the bar. Kelly turned toward Jack to say something but he beat her to it, "So, he really doesn't have an alibi at all. His alibi was trash."

Kelly paused and rethought what she had been about to say. Instead she just said, "I guess it is a little shallow for an alibi, but if Frank really was that drunk he couldn't have hauled those women up into the tree. He probably would have just come back here and passed out."

Jack stared at her a moment. She couldn't really believe this guy was innocent, could she? All he could think to say was, "Let's go back to the station and call it a night. Frank will keep until in the morning. We should get a good night's sleep and start in fresh tomorrow morning."

Kelly was quiet on the car ride back to the station. Jack hoped it was because of the long day. It wasn't every day you had to draw a gun as a detective. Jack had only drawn his twice and both times he had to use it. He was glad that

Kelly hadn't had to use hers. He was feeling very satisfied with the day. They had locked up a dangerous criminal and soon they would be able to find enough evidence to lock him away for good. He suddenly felt like celebrating.

"Want to go for a drink?" Jack asked Kelly.

Kelly seemed to snap awake, "No, thanks, there is something I need to do."

"Okay, I'll see you in the morning, bright and early," Jack said, despondently, as he let her out by her own car.

Kelly unlocked her car and got in. Jack drove off right away, probably to go out and have a beer. Kelly sat in her car for a minute. Leaning back in her seat she closed her eyes and took a few deep breaths. Calming her mind was a difficult trick, but she accomplished it after only a few breaths.

It had been a busy day, but the more she thought about it the more she was sure they had the wrong guy locked up. It was also obvious that the only way she was going to convince Jack of this was if she could present her arguments in a reasonable fashion. It wasn't even five yet so she had some time to figure out her plan of attack. She could figure something out and after that call Jack before he went to bed.

As she quietly sat in her car a plan began to develop. She pursued the idea relentlessly, until she had it firmly in mind. It had a few risks involved, but nothing she couldn't handle. She sat up and turned the key in the ignition.

The wicked man had cursed when he woke from his nap. Too much time had passed. He hurried to his car hoping he would be able to catch her getting off work. If he didn't he wasn't sure how he would find her in time.

His non-descript car pulled up outside the station and stopped. Traffic had been with him and he had arrived 10 minutes before she normally got off. He sunk down into his seat hoping to be less noticeable. Crouched there hiding, he remembered a time when a young man had done the same.

He had pulled up a block short of the house, knowing that if she were home he would be able to tell from there. Hoping it wasn't there, but knowing it might be, he looked for her car. It was there. His heart sank. He was an hour late already, if he waited the punishment would be worse. About to shift back into drive and go face her he stopped as she stepped out of the house.

She was dressed up, as if for work, but it was too late to go to work, besides her work was better done in secret, in her house. Her work involved him sometimes... he shuddered to even think about that. Sometimes he would bleed for days and the kind of men she had for 'clients'... better not to think about it. Quickly he shifted into drive as she pulled away from the curb and started toward the house. He would have to go in and get what he needed and be away before she came back.

As the boy stepped out of the car and started up the steps the man pulled away, disconnecting from what he knew would come. He could pull back his emotions, pull up and out, but not away. The man wanted to look away, but he couldn't. A whimper tore loose from his gut and out through his lips. He wanted to scream, to stop the boy, but nothing he could do now would change the past. Silently, the man watched the boy open the door. Followed the boy into the house. Watched him shut the door. Saw the large hairy, well-muscled arm wrap around the boys throat. Saw the knife. Heard the clothes ripped of the boy...

When the man was able to pull his attention back to the street, he was parked on, and the traffic outside, he was gulping huge lungfuls of air. Looking around frantically he hoped he hadn't missed her.

He needn't have worried. She drove right by him, without so much as glancing in his direction. A deranged smile broke his face – she was alone!

He started his car and followed her. When she got out of her car again he would be ready. He would have his answers.

Chapter Nine

Five minutes later she was pulling into the CU Library parking lot. It was kind of a long shot, but maybe the women had been students here in the past few years. Kelly would spend an hour looking in the yearbooks before she went to outline her plan for Jack. That hour would give him time to eat and get home, she hoped.

She parked as close as she could get to the library, in the interest of saving time. She had to nose in slowly to give the group of students loitering in the parking lot time to move out of her way. Locking her car up, she excused her way through the group and made it the short distance to the library quickly.

The frustrated man cursed his luck again. There were too many people around to stop her here. He pulled into a parking space a few spaces away from her car. He growled under his breath as he watched her, so close, but unreachable, walk into the library.

He waited for a few minutes, but now that he had her license plate he didn't feel the urgency to keep his eyes on her. He could find her again later, even if she left the library before he got back. He had an errand to run. He had an itch that needed scratched and he could take care of that while he waited to catch up to his detective.

The library was quiet. Kelly pretty much had the place to herself. She strode over to the librarian and asked, "Can you tell me where the year books are?"

"Yes, they are in the upstairs stacks. Here I'll write down the exact location for you," the librarian volunteered helpfully. "Just go up the main stairs over there, and turn right. It's the first row," she added pointing toward a big central staircase.

Notepaper in hand and a general idea of which way to go, Kelly went to find the year books. Kelly figured she had about enough time to look through five years' worth. The women looked older than new graduates. They also looked like professionals, not like college students. They'd probably been out of school for a while. Kelly decided to work backwards, starting five years ago. She reasoned that it was likely they could have stayed in Boulder after graduating from CU; quite a few students did that. Boulder was a thriving community and a happening place.

After thirty minutes Kelly was tired of flipping pages. She had a sudden idea and hopped up to go talk to the librarian, leaving the yearbooks on the table.

"Are there any pictures of the students from past years, on the computers?" Kelly asked the librarian. "My fingers are tired of turning pages in the yearbooks," she added, smiling and waiting for an answer.

"Sure, I'll get you started on these computers over here," the librarian said leading Kelly over to a row of computers sitting on a table. There were eight computers in all on the table. Not very private but space efficient. The computers were set up in rows of four and back to back. Kelly was glad no one else was using the computers. She liked her privacy when doing research. Ah, well nothing for it, but to hope no one else wanted to use the computers.

"Thank you" Kelly said. She settled herself at a computer on the farthest end away from the librarian station. She looked pointedly at the librarian waiting for her to leave. The librarian must have thought she didn't know what to do. Kelly knew it was silly to feel that way, especially because the librarian already knew what she was looking for. It was just something that was hardwired into Kelly. She always felt like she was being evaluated, appraised.

The librarian bent over to pull up a site and said, "If you need the internet you can use it here, like you would at home, but some sites are blocked. You might want to do a search on Microsoft Live to find class lists. Often they have pictures of the students in the class."

Kelly pulled in her chair and checked her watch. Only 20 minutes left. It seemed this might have been a waste of time, but she was determined to see it through to the end. She reminded herself a lot could happen in twenty minutes. In twenty minutes your whole life could be turned upside down. In twenty minutes your life could be taken from you. You could lose everything you thought you loved. Yes, twenty minutes could mean everything. With effort Kelly stopped herself from reliving that night. She dragged her morbid thoughts back to the task at hand, more determined than ever to make the best use of this time. She cracked the knuckles of both hands and started surfing the web.

Jack shouldn't have been surprised when Kelly refused to have a drink with him. He wasn't even sure why he offered. Well, actually, if he were totally honest he knew why he had wanted to have drinks with her, just not why the offer had made its way out of his mouth. He hoped, on some level, that they could have gotten drunk enough to continue that kiss. Maybe even take it to the next level. He felt like a heel for even thinking of getting her drunk.

What was he going to do with these feelings? When Jack couldn't think straight he liked to work out, but he was hungry too. Jack decided he would need to eat something before he worked out. Maybe some food would help him decide how to get his emotions back on an even keel.

Jack opened the refrigerator. It was pretty empty. He saw yesterday's soy bean casserole, made with whole wheat noodles. Beside that there was a container of yogurt. On the shelf above was his milk, only raw milk from the farmer's market for him, not pasteurized or reduced fat. Beside the milk was a loaf of bread; he had made it two days before, but it was still plenty fresh.

He opened the hydrator and found only a few fruits in it: an orange, a handful of grapes, and a banana. The drawer below that held his sandwich meat and cheeses. He had fresh hand pulled turkey and roast beef. There were also two choices of cheese: cheddar or Colby. Jack considered his options. He didn't want to eat too much because he was determined to work out hard. Too much food always cramped his stomach.

Jack settled on a bowl of yogurt with fruit cut up in it. He found some of his special homemade granola in the cabinet and added that to the yogurt to give it a bit of crunch. Jack took the whole bowl and his favorite spoon to the dining room table. He preferred to eat his meals on the couch, but when he did that he would sometimes doze off. Today he needed to think and to stay awake for some good, hard exercise.

Jack carefully ate his yogurt, not hurrying; not purposefully dragging it out either. He was worried about Kelly. Why were his feelings still so strong for her? Why couldn't he think about her without wanting to touch her?

His hands ached to feel her hair, to caress her breasts. He couldn't help himself and he moaned a little at the thought of her in his arms, skin on skin, and her breath on his neck. Another part of him just wanted her to cuddle in his arms. He wanted to protect her and comfort her. It was the strangest feeling. He had never wanted that before. That level of intimacy had been foreign to him since that night ten years ago.

He had certainly felt lust before. The sensation of his manhood swelling in his pants to the point where it demanded release was not foreign to him. But this need to comfort, to protect, that was very strange. He wasn't sure he liked it. It stuck him as being what drug addicts must feel when they just had to have another hit of ecstasy. He couldn't stop thinking about her.

The second site Kelly's query pulled up had class photos. Kelly clicked on the link to the evening classes' page for business strategy before she realized it was the evening classes instead of the day classes. She was about to hit the back arrow when a photo caught her eye. It was of a woman with shoulder length auburn hair and blue eyes.

The woman looked a lot like one of the women at Chautauqua Park. Even the sports jacket seemed to be the same. Kelly got excited, but she couldn't be sure they were the same. Could she? Kelly looked closer. Sure enough, names were listed for the students. Kelly shook her head a little at the lack of privacy in the world today.

Acting on impulse she pulled out her cell phone and called information. In response to the automated voice she said "Boulder, Colorado," and after a small pause she added, "Samantha Dargood."

She listened a minute and said, "Please connect me." She loved the fact she didn't even have to write down the number. She knew it would be texted to her phone if she needed it later.

Kelly tucked a strand of hair behind her ear while she waited to see if Samantha was home.

"Hello," a young female voice answered the phone.

"Hello, Samantha?" Kelly asked hopefully. Kelly both wanted the voice on the other end of the phone to be Samantha and she didn't. She wanted her to be Samantha because she hated the idea of the beautiful young woman, full of life being one of the women they found dead.

However, if it wasn't Samantha, Kelly could put her plan into action, the one she was solidifying even now. If the voice on the phone wasn't Samantha, then Samantha might be dead. If Samantha was one of the dead women it would add weight to her plan. Kelly really hoped the voice was Samantha. Suddenly it didn't seem like such a great thing to figure out who these women were. It made it a bit more personal.

"No, she hasn't been here for a couple of days," replied the voice.

"Oh, when do you expect her back please?"

"I'm not sure. I didn't know she was going anywhere and her boss called today to see if she was alright. I'm getting a bit worried about her."

"Have you reported her missing yet?"

"No, do you think I should?" the voice wanted to know.

"Well, is it common for her to go missing for several days at a time?" Kelly really wanted off the phone now that she had the information she needed, but she supposed she should be thorough.

"No, she isn't at all like that. She always tells me where she is going and when she will be back. She didn't come home from class a couple nights ago. I didn't think much about it at the time. I just figured she finally found a guy, you know? Anyway, the next morning she didn't come home, and I couldn't get her to answer her phone. But you know it wasn't that alarming because she had classes so she couldn't answer…"

"Yes, I understand. I really do think you should report it to the police," Kelly interrupted.

"Okay I can do that as soon as we hang up. Can I take a message for you, so I can give it to her when she comes home?"

"No, I think I will try back tomorrow. Thanks and good luck," Kelly said and hung up the phone. She made a mental note to have patrol get a statement tomorrow. She didn't have much hope that Samantha would turn up. Kelly was pretty sure she knew where Samantha was—on a slab in the morgue.

Jack took his bowl to the sink. Rinsing it first, he set it in the dish washer. After glancing around to make sure every-thing was clean and neat he turned out the light and left the kitchen. His workout room was downstairs. He used to go to a club, but soon he discovered he could motivate himself. He preferred to work out in the privacy of his own home. He had installed mirrors on the walls, not out of vanity, but so that he could observe his motions. He wanted each repetition to be completely correct.

Jack wasn't a perfectionist, but where his body was con-cerned he reasoned that he might need every bit of strength he had. He wanted to treat his body the best he could so it wouldn't let him down when he needed it. Jack believed that you are what you eat, but more than that he believed that you are what you do, that nothing comes easy and everything must be worked for.

He started with warm ups. A bit of jogging in place and some stationary bike time got his muscles warmed up. He stretched a bit too. He knew plenty of other men who didn't bother to stretch, but Jack wanted his muscles long and his reactions fast. After a few straddle leg stretches where he could almost do the splits he turned his attention to his shoul-ders. He shrugged them a few times and rotated them for-ward and back, then backward and forward in big circles and little. Finally, when his nerves were screaming for him to do some heavy lifting, he finished by reaching first one hand behind his back, then the other. Each time he used the other hand to help him stretch out his triceps.

Jack looked at his watch, read 6:30 and realized he had warmed up for about 15 minutes. Enough was enough. He sat on the bench, facing the mirror and watched as his arm flexed over and over again, lifting 50 pounds on each curl. He switched arms and did it again. Jack liked to keep his muscles fit. He didn't mind at all that he looked good with his smooth, hard abs and muscles that could turn any girl's head. But he didn't want to be so bulky he had trouble buying clothes. It was a fine balance. Tonight he needed to get a hard enough workout in to forget about Kelly.

As thoughts of her crept into his head he pushed himself harder. By the time he switched from arm muscle sets to leg sets he was lifting more than his usual and lifting it for more reps. Jack actually had to stop himself from loading 500 pounds on his leg press. He normally went for 300 pounds, but today he cranked it up to 450 pounds. Even that didn't seem to be enough.

With every stroke of his legs he imagined stroking Kelly's body. The idea of her under his hard body and his hard body in her was driving him crazy. Jack thrust harder and faster trying to get the image out of his head. When his legs were shaking and he was afraid he would hurt himself if he continued he let the weights come down, shaking the room with a resounding crash.

The whoosh of blood from his head to his toes when he stood up was testament to the fact he was rushing too much. Jack grabbed the side of the machine to steady himself while his world went black for a moment. His low blood pressure didn't like this abuse. Jack didn't care. He walked to the pull up bar, grabbed on, and started pulling himself up over and over again. He didn't stop until he couldn't do any more. Finally Jack sat on the mat with his head in his hands gasping for air. He was totally drained. It had helped a little bit, but only because he was so tired he could hardly think.

Jack grabbed a towel and headed upstairs to get a shower. He cranked the water up to full heat and let it beat at his back and head. The water rushed over his naked body. The sensation was more than he could bear. His erection was starting again and he had to decide what to do about it. He reached down to grab himself, but stopped. It wasn't what he really needed. What he really craved was a Kelly fix. Jack felt it would be wrong to satisfy himself like that. He wasn't at all sure he could handle the emotional backlash, besides if the condition persisted he could always relieve himself in bed later. Instead of completing the contact with his manhood he reached out and turned the water to cold Jack gasped as the freezing water hit his skin.

Chapter Ten

Kelly turned her attention back to the computer and in the next ten minutes located the other three girls, or so she thought. There were actually seven or eight that could have fit the description. All of them were in accelerated night classes. Kelly found a couple women in each class that might have been the ones murdered, but Kelly felt that some were too tall or too short. Some didn't have blue eyes. Her final criterion wasn't very sound, but she knew the killer was looking for something specific. She narrowed it down by guessing that they all had to be from separate classes. The killer was smart and would probably realize that two missing women from a single class it would draw more suspicion. Kelly printed some of the information, including color pictures.

Kelly checked her watch. Her hour was over. She packed up her notes, closed down the computer connection and grabbed her coat. "Do you have the night class schedule?" she asked the librarian as she left. She flipped through the handout on the way to her car. There was only one class that

night and it started at 8:00 pm. Kelly needed to be in that
class for her plan to work.

The sky was already dim when Kelly left the library. She
hated how early it got dark in the winter months in Colorado.
The silver paint on her Chrysler Crossfire was muted by the
darkening sky. Kelly climbed into the driver's seat and set
her stuff in the passenger seat. Carefully, she pulled out of
the parking space and headed straight to Jack Hall's house.

She had a plan and she had to make him see reason about
this. They had the wrong guy and Kelly knew the killer
would strike again. Kelly intended to stop the murderer this
time, with or without Jack's help.

*The man raced back toward the library with his errand
completed. It had taken longer than he thought. Two more
times the boy had occupied his thoughts to the exclusion
of all else. He hated the boy, even more than he hated the
woman. No, that wasn't true, was it? Not quite. He hated
that the boy had been so weak. So helpless before the
woman. If the boy had not been so weak, the woman would
have loved him more. She would have been prouder of
him, less angry with him. No, that wasn't right either... he
just couldn't put his finger on it.*

*He was distracted enough by his own churning
thoughts that he almost didn't see her driving toward him.
His head snapped over his left shoulder following the
movement of her car as he made sure it was her. For a
minute it had looked like the woman from his past; the
woman the boy knew.*

He quickly popped a U-turn at the next intersection and followed her. This time he would get his satisfaction. A deep throated laugh escaped him. Even he could hear the edge of madness in it, but this time, maybe for the first time in his life, the sound didn't disturb him.

He tailed her to a house. There wasn't much parking on the street. She took the only space for a block. By the time he circled the block and parked, she was standing at the door to a house, ringing the bell with a frustrated look on her face. The man got out of his car and started toward her.

When the house door opened, he quickly ducked behind a tree, cursing as his prey eluded him again. He back-tracked to his car, waiting silently for her to reappear.

The night air smelled of pine with an uncommonly warm fall breeze. Kelly paused outside Jack's house for a moment and gathered her thoughts. She had to be professional. Any longing to renew their teen love affair would have to be ignored. Jack had been clear about that. He wouldn't sleep with her, either because of professional pride, or, more likely, because he really didn't feel for her the way she felt for him. Kelly reminded herself yet again she was not fit to be his lover. Tucking an errant strand of hair behind one ear she squared her shoulders and strode briskly up to his door, she wasn't here for sex.

Pausing only long enough to take a deep breath, she rang the bell. She hoped he wouldn't take it the wrong way that she was here after work hours. Kelly didn't want him to think she would try to make advances after he had made his position so crystal clear.

Jack took a long time to get to the door. It gave Kelly plenty of time to think. Was it such a good idea to spring this on him tonight? It could wait till tomorrow morning when they could talk about it in the light of day. Maybe she should give them more time to plan for this adventure of hers. They should have backup, and that would be hard to get this time of night. No, she was resolved to see this through and to stop the murderer before he could strike again.

Oh, where was Jack? What was taking him so long? Kelly raised her hand to ring the bell again, but paused. What if he had a woman with him?

The doorbell rang while he was in the shower. Thinking it was one of the neighbors needing to borrow something he grabbed a towel and dashed to the door. Instead of his neighbor, Kelly stood on his porch.

The doorbell must have caught him in the shower. His hair was wet, hanging in little ringlets on his forehead. Water dripped down his shoulders and onto his bare chest. Her eyes followed the lines of his body. His chest was tan with a light dusting of hair. One light scar teased her eyes lower till she was gazing at his six pack abs. Not a bit of fat on him, she thought. Her eyes followed the rippling muscles down the cascade that was his stomach.

Kelly was definitely disappointed when her view was interrupted by the blue terry cloth towel wrapped around his waist. The towel was thick and warm and made Kelly wonder if what it hid was thick and warm too. Kelly felt herself start to blush. Quickly she averted her gaze. She looked back up at his face. His quick smile, when he saw her made him look mischievous. If he made a move for her there was no way she would resist. She just wouldn't be that strong.

The way her eyes traveled down his hard body he knew she wanted him. She seemed surprised by what she saw. An hour a day in his home gym kept him in perfect shape. He gave her plenty of time to get a good long look. When her eyes finally met his again, he grinned.

He couldn't very well leave her standing on his porch while he went to change, "Come on in," he invited.

"Thanks," she said stepping through the open door. On the way by him she brushed up against his towel and it almost came loose. Was that an accident, he wondered? Did he wish it had slipped off? He felt another erection brush the towel. He was definitely going to be embarrassed by his reaction soon, if he didn't get back in the shower and turn it to full cold, again.

Kelly accidently caught her hand on the towel as she brushed past him. The shock of that little contact told her that she was lost. There was no way she would be able to leave without feeling all of him. She kept walking as she heard the door close behind her. All plans that she had worked up in her head had fled. The only plan that mattered, right now, was one that would get her into bed with Jack. She had to release the heat building between her legs, threatening to burn through her like a fever. Kelly clasped both hands together and held them at her waist. She knew they would shake if she didn't anchor them.

He turned to look at her back walking into his house. She had the perfect shape. Smooth hips, tight waist, firm breasts and legs that went on forever. He wanted to know if she still felt as good on him, next to him, around him. He couldn't resist.

Jack reached out and caught her arm spinning her around to face him. Her breath caught in her throat and her mind went on hold. He pulled her into his arms ferociously. Like a dying man in the desert he drank in her lips. Kissing, exploring, and begging with his tongue.

The initial kiss was so hard her mouth felt bruised, but she didn't mind. After a moment he slowed down as if he were afraid of hurting her. She opened her mouth to encourage him in deeper. She wanted to taste all of him. Every inch was important to her questing tongue and mouth. The kiss lingered a long time.

She pulled her mouth away from his. Starting down his neck and chest with her lips, she absorbed the taste of him. Kelly moved lower. The towel lay forgotten on the floor. She was ready to sink all the way down and take him into her mouth right there in the kitchen.

He knew he would lose it right there is she went down on him. He couldn't embarrass himself like that. He wanted to take control again, to slow it down a bit so he could pleasure her. He pulled her up and, looking into her eyes, swept her into his arms.

Suddenly she was in his arms again, cradled against his chest, just like ten years before. After a surprised moment she laid her head on his chest and relaxed. His capable arms held her tight as he carried her up the stairs to his bedroom. Breathing only slightly hard, he set her tenderly on his bed.

There were a hundred things she should say. None of them came out of her mouth. In truth she really didn't want to push him away. She needed him. She wanted to be made love to again. It had been too long since her husband died. But she wouldn't think about that right now. She wouldn't think about anything. She didn't have to think to feel.

Jack gently bent over her, his lips brushing hers tentatively. Just the lightest touch. He pulled back and Kelly was afraid he would back down again, but his eyes just held a question. Not trusting herself to talk Kelly pulled him down to her again. This time she opened her mouth and teased his tongue into hers. He tasted heavenly, slightly sweet from his dinner, yet salty from his workout.

Her hands wrapped into his hair pulling him down tighter against her. She deepened the kiss. His arms collapsed so he was supporting his weight on his elbows. Kelly could feel his crotch bulge between them. It was like a rock pushing into her thigh. He rocked ever so slightly against her, his hard shaft massaged her upper leg and hip joint.

She could hear his moans. Frustration surfaced and made her that much hornier. She ran her hands down his strong back to his firm, naked buttocks. He was undressed and yet clothes separated them still. She had to feel his skin on hers. She brought her questing hands to his chest and pushed for him to get up, to release her from her clothes... She had to touch him, feel him against her bare breasts, wrap herself around him.

Jack thought it was a bit comical that he was undressed, yet Kelly was fully clothed. Their kisses deepened until he was hard as a rock. He could feel his rod pushing at the cloth that separated them. He wiggled a little, her rough pants stimulating his sex. Shots of pleasure raced up his body making him moan out loud. He needed to slow down or he would embarrass himself. This had to be leisurely. He had to take his time, not rush it.

Her hands were pushing him away, but she wasn't saying no. Just the opposite, she pulled his hand onto her breast and ground her pelvis into his. He pulled back, breaking contact with her body. She groaned as if he had physically hurt her. Yes, Jack wanted to take this very slow. He started with her shoes and made sure she got a long look at his naked body while he did it.

Kelly was surprised at the intensity of loss she felt when Jack pulled away from her. The lack of contact left her body aching. She wanted him and she wanted him now! She didn't have time to draw this out. He body was demanding him. Her sex ached to feel him deep within her. He was beautiful standing over her. He slowly pulled off her shoes. His rock hard body teased her with its erection straining toward her.

With a frustrated gasp she reached down and unbuttoned her pants. Ignoring the zipper, she jerked them down about her ankles, quickly worming her feet out of them. He reached down to help, but she'd already yanked her feet free. She grabbed his arms and pulled him down onto her.

Jack wanted to take it slow. He wanted to kiss her tender spots, to make love to her like she deserved. He wanted to worship her body. Now, lying on top of her chest, he couldn't stand not feeling all of her. Pushing up just a little, he tried to get her shirt off. Leaning over onto one elbow he worked one of her arms loose. The shirt tangled her hands over her head, but he freed it quickly. The things she had been doing to his body with those hands were wonderful. He couldn't be deprived of their touch.

Kelly had one arm free and she desperately wanted the other. Her body ached with its need. She had to get her clothes off. She wanted to feel all of him and she wanted it now. Hurry, Jack, you're making me crazy, she thought. He was taking his own time dragging his tongue along her exposed side.

Leisurely he gently pushed her bra up, exposing one breast. His tongue played over the smooth skin of her side and breast. When his lips brushed her nipple she moaned and her hands grabbed for him, shoving hard. Suddenly he was on his back, Kelly straddling him as her shirt and bra flew off the bed. As Kelly thrust herself onto him Jack gave up on taking it slow.

Kelly mounted him, she was taking the lead. No more of his slow torture, she had to have him now. She thrust her weight down on his strutting shaft, swallowing the whole of it into her moistness. Over and over again she rose upon him. In and out. The depth of her emotions matched the depth of his shaft. She felt him moving with her, his thrusting increasing its rhythm.

Every stroke teased her sex. Every time he rubbed over her button, she felt like she would cum, only to have the sensation flee until his next stroke. She was always on the edge and never allowed to cross over. It was like looking at heaven through the pearly gates, but not being allowed in. She thought she would explode.

Jack couldn't hold on much longer. Kelly was driving him crazy, her movements and little moans too much for him to ignore. He was so swollen he would rip through her if he didn't explode soon. Suddenly she shifted her movements, clamping upon him like a vice. She was so tight.

Kelly shifted her movements to try to get relief. She was going crazy with the need to orgasm. It was sweet, exquisite torture. She clenched her butt muscles and tightened her sex. She felt Jack respond to her tightness. A little gasp for air revealed that he liked what she was doing.

Suddenly she knew it was time. All she had to do was reach for it and the orgasm would come. It was a relief to be holding it back instead of searching for it. She wanted this orgasm to be intense. She needed Jack to feel how much she wanted him. She let her weight settle onto him, grinding with her desire. She felt him pulse within her, sending her over the edge into her own ecstasy. Her back arched with the force of it. She collapsed on him and lay still. He felt so right.

Jack wrapped his arms around Kelly. It felt so right to be inside of her. Now his erection was slowly fading; any minute he would slip from her. He could wait for it. She was light against his chest, hardly any weight at all.

Kelly broke the embrace first. She pulled away and straightened her legs. She lay down beside him and stroked the fur on his chest. Her eyes traced his body from his spent manhood up his chest to his face. He had the most handsome face. She was definitely still in love with this man. Her focus softened as she looked at his face, her thoughts drifting everywhere and nowhere.

When her eyes refocused she was looking at the clock. Oh, no, it was already 7:15. She only had a half hour to explain her plan. That would leave only fifteen minutes to drive to campus and get into the classroom. "Jack, we have to talk," she said.

Jack rolled toward her, stirring from his peaceful half-awake state, "Hmmm, no we don't have to talk now. It can wait till morning."

"No, Jack I have a plan to catch the real murderer."

"Kelly, we went over this once already. We have the real murderer. Frank is in jail. Case closed. We deserve some rest and relaxation for solving this case so fast." Jack really wished she would just relax and do some more of what they had been doing. He reached for her.

Kelly was annoyed. She really wanted to crawl back into bed with Jack, curl up and forget the nightmare they had been living for the last two days. She just couldn't do it. Couldn't he see this was hard enough for her without making it more difficult? She had already given in to her body's needs once this day; now she had to think with her head.

"Jack, just listen to me, okay?" Kelly said this forcefully enough to stop his wandering hands.

Sitting up in bed, Jack said, "Okay, you have my attention. First let's assume you are right and we don't have the right guy. Why can't this wait till morning?"

Oh, boy, she hadn't planned on having to tell him this right now. Nothing for it now, except to go ahead. "I have to tell you this. I have to...let me start again, okay?" At his nod Kelly tried again, "My husband, Paul, was a good man. He took good care of me and didn't deserve to die. It was my fault he died."

Jack started to protest, but Kelly cut him off, "Please, just let me finish."

It looked like this was going to be very difficult for Kelly. Jack really didn't want to hear about her ex-husband, particularly now. It spoiled the moment. But if she had to tell this story, he would listen. However, he was not at all happy with her blaming herself for Paul's death. Jack would keep quiet, as she asked, but when she was done he would make love to her. Then she would forget this nonsense. He schooled his face to impassiveness and just listened.

"There was a serial murderer in our town in Ohio. My husband bought me a gun; a very small 9 mm that fit easily into my purse. You see, I was working long hours at the office. Often I had to stay at work late, and Paul worried I might be in danger when I left work at night. He offered to come pick me up every night, but I refused. He had to work early hours and I didn't want him sleep deprived."

Jack wondered where Kelly was going with all of this. He knew Paul was dead and he was sorry to hear it, but he really didn't want to think about the intricacies of Kelly's marriage. Jack struggled to pay attention and not tune her out as she continued.

"Paul bought me the gun a few weeks before they apprehended the killer. I was never comfortable carrying it in my purse, especially without a permit." Kelly paused a minute to catch her breath, and to get her courage up for the next part of the story, the worst part. Now that she had started talking she couldn't stop. Kelly could feel the tears building behind her eyes. If she paused too long they would burst forth and she wouldn't be able to finish. She had to finish. Jack had to know the truth about her, no matter what the cost.

"Well, the murderer never tried to attack me. In fact he didn't manage to kill anyone else in the ensuing weeks before the police caught him. The night we learned they had him in custody I demanded Paul let me put the gun away. I wasn't even sure I could use it if I had to. Paul agreed, but he didn't want to sell it. We didn't have any kids so it was not that unsafe to have it in the house. Paul talked me into keeping it in the front hall closet. We stored it way up high, under the family pictures."

Kelly paused again. Jack was getting more and more concerned. What could have happened? Had she shot her husband by accident? Maybe he had shot himself and she was blaming herself for keeping the gun. Jack no longer had to struggle to pay attention. He held his breath, waiting for her to finish.

"We had just put the gun up when there was a knock at the door," Kelly continued. "Paul answered it, and a man came in. When I saw that the guy he let in had a machete behind his back, I panicked. I hid in the closet, the same closet the gun was in." Now Kelly sped up her story, she wanted to get it out. The words were taking on a life of their own as she relived the moment. She couldn't have stopped their flow any more than she could change the events that had happened that awful night. "The murderer didn't give Paul time to even call for help. Paul never even screamed. The killer cut him down in the front hallway, while I looked on through the door of the closet. It happened so fast I didn't even have time to get the gun out. I was too scared to move, and thought he would hear and kill me too."

Jack held her hand, stunned. By now Kelly was sobbing. "What happened?" he asked.

"He left," Kelly said. "It was an hour before I could bring myself to come out of the closet. I forgot all about the gun." She paused again. "And when I came out, there was Paul's body…" she choked up and stopped again.

"I thought you said the killer had been caught?"

"Paul and I didn't know it, but that night the police had to let the murderer go."

Jack couldn't help it he interrupted, "What!" It was more of an exclamation than a question.

"Yes, they said that they had made a mistake with his arrest." Kelly's sobs slowed as she tried to get control of herself. "The news wasn't specific, but later I found out that some of the evidence had been misplaced. One of the officers had also gotten rough with the guy when he was arresting him. Add it all together and it meant the murderer could go free."

Jack was not sure what to do. He didn't think this was her fault, but he also was quickly coming to the realization that she was still trying to come to grips with Paul's death. She was trying to find comfort and acceptance from someone, because she couldn't give it to herself. He couldn't let himself be used that way. She needed help and it was help he couldn't give. She obviously needed a therapist. Maybe she could start with the department therapist. He wasn't sure how she had gotten through the academy with this level of trauma and misperception. There was no way he was qualified to help her with this.

He resented the used feeling overcoming him. She hadn't really wanted him. He was just the first place she had looked for attention since Paul's death. His first reaction was anger, but he pulled that under control because he couldn't really blame her. Jack had loved her in high school and he guessed he still loved her on some level. Her pain made him sad. He couldn't help her directly, never the less he had to do something. He took her into his arms saying, "There was nothing you could have done."

This stopped her tears. How could he say there was nothing she could have done? She could have, should have, gone for the gun. She should have burst from the closet and stopped the guy or died trying. Her inaction caused a good man to die. It was her fault. She couldn't believe Jack didn't see this. "How could you not understand? I should have done something. I should have moved faster. I could have stopped it. I should have used the gun."

Jack didn't have anything left to say. There was no way he could convince her it wasn't her fault. If she had tried to stop it, she would be dead too. Jack opted to just pull her close again, "I'm sorry," was all he could think to say. He knew it wasn't enough. He wasn't sure what would be enough, but tomorrow morning he would try to find out where she could go.

Catching her breath, the sobs stopped, Kelly pushed on, "Well I didn't mean to break down and lay all that on you, but I had to make you see why this is so important to me."

"I understand, but Frank is locked up for the night. He can't get out. We have enough evidence to put him away or at least hold him a long time. He is not getting loose." Was Kelly so messed up over this that she couldn't see the difference between the cases? Jack was getting more concerned by the minute. Maybe he could just talk her back into bed for the night. Tomorrow would be a new day. He could worry about it all tomorrow.

"Don't you see, if the detectives had done their job, Paul would be alive? If we do our jobs we might prevent another death. I have a plan to catch the real killer. I just need some support." Kelly saw Jack's look of disbelief and she hurried on to get her plan out before he could interrupt her. "I want to pose as one of the women and catch the guy when he tries to take me. I figured out who the women were. They were all taking various night classes at CU in the business school."

"Wait a minute. You figured out who they are? How did you do that? Did you find a missing person report that I missed?"

"No, I had a crazy idea and I followed up on it. I looked at pictures from current classes at night school. All the women were taking accelerated night classes in the business school at CU. I don't have time to explain how I found out who they are. My class starts in," she paused to look at the clock, "20 minutes. Either you trust me on this one and back me up or I will go alone."

Jack was tired. He was fast losing patience with this whole thing. He didn't even feel like inviting her back to bed anymore. Kelly obviously had more psychological problems than a hornets' nest had stingers. He had no idea why Kelly was obsessing over this. Actually, he guessed he did have a good idea after what she had told him about her husband. Jack remembered his first time at a homicide. He had felt so powerless. He hadn't even been there at the time it happened. He was only investigating it, but he remembered wanting so badly to catch the guy. But this was totally different. They had the bad guy in jail right now. He couldn't hurt anyone else, as least not if they kept doing their job right. There was no doubt that he was guilty. Jack would find the evidence to put him away for life.

Jack could see Kelly waiting for a response from him. He didn't have a good one. He wanted to believe she was fine and that she would snap out of this self-reproach tomorrow. But right now it just looked, to him, like she was crazy. He was not up to dealing with this. He would report it to the police department therapist in the morning. For right now her delusions were not his problem.

He would not give them more credence by playing along. He was tired and wanted nothing more than to lie back down in bed and collapse till morning. All of his desire for her had been pushed to the back of his head by the realization she was this traumatized. He didn't need that kind of relationship. He'd let his memories of that one night blind him. Kelly was obviously a different person now. He should have never given in to his urges. Maybe the therapist would get her reassigned to a different partner.

"Kelly, I can't deal with this tonight. I will check your leads on the dead women's identities tomorrow, but for tonight I just want to go to bed," just to be clear he added, "by myself."

Kelly was crushed. They had just made passionate wonderful love. Now he was treating her like she was crazy. And that last comment was just way out of line. It was like a total rejection. Had he not felt anything she had? While his hands were on her and he was in the throes of his orgasm he had certainly responded as if he had enjoyed it.

Maybe he was just really tired. She wasn't sure she could do it by herself. All of her training screamed at her, 'you need your partner!' She would try one last time to get him to help her. Kelly took a deep breath putting all her reserve and calmness into her voice, she pleaded, "Jack, I have to do this. I am not sure at all that Frank is the murderer; scum, trash and gross yes, but not a murderer."

Now Jack was really angry. He had nine years more experience than she did. She had been on the job for all of 2 days and she thought she knew more than he did. This was crazy, "Kelly, just leave! Go Home! I will see you in the morning and we deal with this." He said it forcefully. He clamped his mouth shut so he wouldn't say anything else that he might regret later.

His words hit her like a tornado, sending her thoughts into chaos. She stumbled blindly from the room, grabbing her clothes as she went. She couldn't believe he had acted that way. Was he that upset about her challenging his findings on the case? If he was, there was truly no hope for them. Ha, how could she think about a 'them' after what he had just said? Should she should just go home and go to bed? Maybe he would see reason in the morning.

Her resolve hardened again. How dare he treat me like that! Like some flighty house wife who can't think on her own! I am trained for this. My hunches should count for something, and besides that they are more than hunches. There was a reasonable doubt, but Jack, with his egotistical attitude, couldn't see it.

There was another reason he might be acting this way. After what Kelly told him he might think she was dangerous or that she couldn't hold up her end in the partnership. Kelly couldn't stand the confirmation that she was tainted. His rejection stung. It was hard enough to accept that he refused to see her side and thought she was too inexperienced to know more than him. It would totally crush her to believe he might think of her as cursed. No, she would not consider that. Jack's rejection had to be based on his belief she was wrong. But a little voice still tickled the back of her mind saying, 'He can't even stand to be around you after what you did to Paul.' She viciously pushed that voice down and refused to listen to it.

She reached dejectedly into her pocket for her car keys and instead came out with the class schedule that she had shoved in there when she formed her plan. Why not go ahead with her plan? She didn't need him. She could do this. If she were wrong it was only her evening she was wasting. But if she were right it was a chance to atone for past mistakes. Nothing would bring Paul back, but maybe stopping another murderer and saving some woman's life would be enough to calm her nightmares. Yes, she would go to class that night. She checked her watch. It was 7:50. She had just enough time to get there.

The impatient man jerked upright in his seat when her car started. He hadn't seen her come out of the house. He started his car and pulled out behind her when she left the neighborhood. He drove automatically less aware of the car in front of him than his own inner turmoil.

The thoughts intruded all the time now. Even if he didn't always see what the boy was doing or thinking he had thoughts about it. It was more than memories, but less than visions. The boy drove after the woman. She had crossed the line and after she had used him along with her three guests his face burned with shame. At 16 he had never had to face that before. In the last 8 years she had never participated along with her other guests, in using him. She had never laid a hand on him, except to punish him for not being strong enough, brave enough, quiet enough, or loud enough to please the constant flow of men who came to her late night sessions.

This time he was angry, and ashamed. He hurt all over and although, he knew he was a man, he felt like a boy. He hated that feeling and was determined to never feel that way again. He would catch her and show her he could be a man,

He would follow her yet again. This time she wouldn't escape. He would have her. She would be powerless against him.

Chapter Eleven

Jack lay in bed looking at the ceiling, hearing Kelly's car door slam as she drove away. He replayed their conversation over and over again. What could he have done differently? The longer he thought about it the more upset he became. He remembered again his first homicide. The feeling of helplessness had overwhelmed him. His first homicide hadn't been anywhere near as premeditated and graphic as these. It was only natural that Kelly would be upset. Between the trauma of her husband's death and the stress of her first two days on the job… well it was no wonder she sounded on edge and about to have a nervous breakdown.

He thought about all her arguments, dissecting each of them, one by one. He had to admit that Kelly had some valid points. It was strange that they didn't find the gun. It was also strange that Frank seemed like scum, but not a murderer. Maybe she had a point. He could at least back her up tonight. He guessed he owed it to her.

Slowly, with growing conviction he got out of bed and put on his clothes. The more he thought about it, the more urgent it seemed that he make sure Kelly didn't do anything dangerous. In her state of mind she could be in danger even without the murderer. She might be a danger to herself. By the time he had finished this thought he was running for his car.

Jack headed for the business school on the main CU campus. He figured he could just walk the buildings until he found one that was still open. That would be where Kelly was, unless she had gone home. If she had gone home chances were she would have calmed down and no longer be a danger to herself. If that was the case he could wait till later to find her.

On the other hand if she were at the school, he could keep quiet and just watch over her. Her plan was so full of holes he didn't really think she was in danger from the killer. He was more concerned about what she would do when the murderer didn't take the bait. Where would her self-doubts take her then?

His reaction to her plan may have pushed her over an edge he hadn't seen, especially since he had been such a heel. He should have pulled his head out of his butt long enough to be more sympathetic. Jack berated himself with every step he took. Thoughts of Kelly doing something stupid pushed his steps until he was almost running.

The shady man watched his detective visit the business school. Why was she there this late at night? Was she tracking him? He giggled manically at the thought of her pursuing him and him pursuing her. The two of them running in circles that would never connect.

Even as he tracked her, his thoughts were elsewhere... the boy saw the woman pull her car into a dirt road; he followed her. She drove up the narrow twisting road. The boy didn't know this road. It was overgrown, but still passable at a decent speed. After miles and miles she stopped the car. He pulled to a stop, and backed up around the last corner he had turned, pulling off the road out of site. Getting out of his car, keeping to the bushes he crept up on the woman.

She was weeping. The boy paused. The knife was in his hand. He was unsure of what to do. He never imagined she wept, not ever. In the end it didn't matter. She screamed in a very satisfactory way as his knife found her eyes first.

In the end it had been easy. He had no trouble blocking out her cries, like she had blocked his for all these years. He wondered why it had taken him so long...but he found no answer.

The detective had been a lot harder to catch alone. Well, this time he had her exactly where he wanted. He knew the school well; catching up, to her, would be easy here. He stepped from his car and walked toward the building into which she had disappeared. His limp was barely noticeable. Now that he was rested, he would be able to keep up. Yes, she would be his before the night was out.

Completely unaware that she was being watched, Kelly parked close to the business school. She made sure to park under a street light and walked quickly to her class. She was always cautious when out late at night on her own. The self-defense classes she had taken at Paul's insistence stuck with her even after his death. The training she received at the academy helped also.

Kelly walked into class only a few minutes late. Everyone turned to look at her when the door snapped shut. Even the teacher stopped talking and stared at her. He looked like he was waiting for something. Kelly managed to stammer an apology, "Sorry, I'm late. I just signed up today," and she smiled to help smooth things over. Hopefully he wouldn't ask for her registration form until after class. Then she could pretend she was in the wrong room all along.

The room was large enough to be tiered. Steps ran down the aisle from the door Kelly had just stepped through, to the podium and chalkboards. Theater seats, filled sporadically with students, lined each side of the stairs.

Kelly estimated there were about 50 students in attendance, the room was maybe half full. She found a seat near the back of the room. She sat silently and pulled out a notebook and pen. Seeing that she was settled into her chair, the teacher resumed his lecture.

Kelly kicked off her shoes, which had been cramping her feet, and pulled off her socks. She wiggled her toes, sighing a little under her breath. The guy sitting next to her grinned, "Long day, huh?" he asked. Kelly smiled at him as she stretched her bare feet out in front of her.

Kelly really didn't pay much attention to the teacher for the first 15 minutes or so of class. Instead she proceeded to make notes about her observations from the case. She was careful to study the students, noting those that seemed out of place or potential targets. There were only two doors out of the room, one down front for the teacher, and no windows.

After observing everything she could, she started paying attention to the teacher.

Forty-five minutes into the lecture Kelly was bored. This was sophomore stuff that she had finished over eight years ago. She knew all about how to start your own company. Unfortunately, the information had not changed much in those years and Kelly did not need a review. Also, to add to her disappointment, no one had shown up who looked like a suspect.

Kelly had to admit this might be a wild goose chase, but with forty-five minutes left in class she could stick it out to make sure. She just needed a break. She looked at the man sitting next to her and said, "Bathroom break," in a quiet voice. She folded her notebook shut; debated putting her shoes on and decided she didn't need them. She would be right back. She left her pack, notebook and pen and she quietly stood up and slipped out the door while the teacher had his back turned.

The concrete hallway was cold on her bare feet. It felt wonderful after being in the dress shoes all day. Well, not quite all day she reflected with a small smile. She had been on her back for some of it, and on her front, too. Kelly's smile disappeared as quickly as it came when those thoughts led to the conclusion of their evening. She didn't want to think about Jack and his motives any more.

She wasn't sure where to go, but she saw a restroom sign down the brightly lit hallway. She decided to walk that way. It was an age old stalling technique from all the way back in grade school. When you are bored or want to get out of work you go to the bathroom. As Kelly's hand touched the door knob to open it she heard a door shut. She jumped and looked around, but she was alone in the hall. Shrugging it off to nerves she went into the utilitarian bathroom.

After washing her hands and rinsing her face she left the bathroom. The hall was still empty. The light from her classroom demanded she return before the teacher missed her. She paused only long enough to get a drink. The water fountain was against the wall. Kelly pulled her hair back behind her ears and leaned over to take a long drink.

Without warning a hand clamped down on her left shoulder. A cloth was pressed over her face. The hand switched from her shoulder to her chest, roughly pulling her up and away from the fountain. The cloth clamped on her face pressed harder. It was over her nose and mouth. She was suffocating. She took a deep breath to scream. At the same time, she lashed out with her foot trying to hit the attacker's instep. She wished for the heels of her shoes that were sitting under her desk.

She had just enough time to think it was a shame she had been right, feel her foot crunch bone, and wish Jack were there before she passed out from the chloroform on the rag that had been shoved in her face.

Jack took longer finding the building than he wanted. His watch read 9:00 pm by the time he found the only lit classroom in the building. He was afraid the class would be over, but it was still in full swing. He stood quietly in the back of the room and let his eyes play over the heads of the students in the room. He saw her in the front row. Her auburn hair shone in the bright fluorescents. He stared at her a moment drinking in the sight.

He longed to run his fingers through that long hair again. To hold it to his face and breathe in the lilac scent of it. Jack had just started to wonder how long he would have to stand in the class and listen to the boring spiel coming out of the teacher's mouth before she would turn around. He wanted to let her know he would support her. He could explain that he couldn't be there for her like a lover again, but that as a partner he could do his half.

When she turned around he smiled right at her. The woman who smiled back wasn't Kelly. Jack looked around confused. He was so sure it had been her. He had wasted several minutes just standing in the classroom, looking at the wrong person. Mentally he berated himself. Where was Kelly if she wasn't here? Could he have missed her? Could she have gone home instead, like he had told her?

He took a deep breath and scanned the classroom one more time. All of the students had their eyes forward, paying close attention to the teacher. He didn't see anyone else that came close to looking like Kelly. She wasn't in the room. Jack gave a mental shrug. He had been pretty sure she was stubborn enough to try to carry out her plan, even without him. Obviously he had been wrong. Maybe she was at home.

He turned to leave. That was when he noticed the notebook and pen sitting alone on a desk in the back of the room. He walked over to the notebook and took a look at the neatly penned notes. Just from the handwriting, before he even read them, he knew they were written by Kelly. Her script he would never forget.

In high school she had passed him note after note. He still remembered the first one. Can we meet after school to talk about the arrangements for homecoming game? It had been simple and to the point, but even then he had hopes. He had read so much more into it than the simple request to talk about preparations for the big game. He had raised it to his nose and taken a deep whiff of her flowery scent.

After that wonderful night she had written him a 'Dear John letter.' He had kept the note for years. He didn't remember where the note was now, but he would never forget the words. She had written, "Dear Jack, You are my life. I love you with all that I am. I will always love you. Even knowing this, I ask your forgiveness. I can't stay here and go to college with you. I have to accept the scholarship. My parents are insistent. I have to listen to my parents. They have much more experience than I do, in the world. I must follow their wishes for now. I hope you understand. I can't bear to see you again, knowing we would have to part. I am leaving for Washington as soon as I mail this letter to you. All my love, Kelly."

Jack had crumpled the note in his hand after reading it three times. How could she leave him? He loved her and she was throwing that away. He had run to the airport, but it had been too late. Her plane was gone. His parents wouldn't hear of him chasing after her. He was to stay and go to CU and take over the family ranch someday. He laughed a little inside, reflecting how that had not gone as planned for his parents. He loved being a detective. Jack was lost in thought. He picked up her notebook to look at it more closely.

The memories were so overpowering that, had the teacher not interrupted, he might have sniffed the notebook paper. "Excuse me, young man, may I help you?" The professor raised his voice from the front of the room to get Jack's attention.

"Hmm, oh. Yes sir, do you know where the woman sitting here went?"

"No idea, but you are interrupting my class, could you please leave?" The professor snapped.

"Actually, I can't leave, she is a detective and my partner," with a long practiced, smooth motion he pulled out his badge. "We are working on a case and I expected her to be here."

The student next to Kelly's seat asked, "Was she a very pretty auburn haired lady?" When Jack nodded his head in affirmation the kid continued, "I saw her leave about 15 minutes ago. I thought she was going to the bathroom, but she didn't come back." For good measure he added, "Can I help look for her?"

Jack declined the help saying, "I am sure she just got called away for an appointment. I'll find her pretty soon." Jack picked up the notebook, and grabbed for the pen. It slipped off the desk and onto the floor. He bent to retrieve it, surprised to see Kelly's shoes and backpack under the desk. Stunned, he rose up too quickly. His head met the underside of the desk with a resounding thud. Jack straightened all the way holding a hand to the back of his head. He shoved her shoes into the backpack along with the notebook. He left the forgotten pen on the floor beneath the desk. Jack scurried from the room before the teacher could do more than scowl at him.

Jack was already half way down the hall before he was even sure about where he was headed. He decided the bathroom was the best choice. Why in the world would she take her shoes off? Then again, he remembered that Kelly had always disliked dress shoes. All the girls at prom had kicked off their shoes to dance, but Kelly was the only one who didn't put them back on to go walking in the park afterward. Jack smiled a little as he remembered that they had to sneak back into school through an open window to retrieve them. The building had been locked up tight. He also remembered those feet. He had kissed them, every inch of them, just as he had done earlier that day. He had to find her.

Jack hoped she would be in the bathroom, but he was far from sure. Maybe she had finally had a break down, and ran for home. There was only one way to find out for sure. He strode down the hall with long sure strides. The women's bathroom was on the left. He knocked on the door. No one answered. He opened the door a crack and called, "Hello?" in a fairly loud voice. Still hearing no answer he walked in, cautiously, lest he disturb some woman at her ministrations. The stalls were empty, except for the one at the end. It was shut and locked. When Jack peeked under the edge of the door he saw a pair of shoes. Jack said, "Uh, excuse me, but I am looking for a young woman." There was no answer from the feet in the stall. "Kelly, are you in there?"

Jack was getting more and more concerned. He didn't stop to think that the feet he saw in the stall had shoes on, but that Kelly's shoes were in the backpack on his shoulder. Making his decision, not really caring anymore if she wanted privacy or was just not responding because she was mad at him, he took a coin out of his pocket. Placing the edge of it in the back of the lock he turned the lock to open the door.

Jack caught a flash of dark brown hair before the purse slammed into his head. There was an accompanying scream to further punish his beat up head. The woman in the stall was definitely not Kelly Swift. He tried to apologize, but the woman was signing frantically, too fast for him to follow. Apparently, she was deaf. Jack roughly signed that he was sorry.

He shut the stall and left the bathroom. Jack was standing outside the restroom trying to decide what to do next when the deaf woman came out. Jack felt his cheeks heat up. He bent over to take a drink from the water fountain to hide his embarrassment. It didn't help much, but he did notice a rag on the ground. He had just started to bend over before the deaf woman tapped him on the shoulder. He straightened, bumping his elbow painfully on the water fountain. One of his more colorful words slipped out of his mouth. His face flamed a hotter red. He didn't like to use foul language in front of women. Even if she couldn't hear it, she could probably read lips.

He looked at her. She was very mad; her hands flying in sharp choppy motions at high speed. He only caught half of what she was saying. He had not had to use his sign language since his mom died two years before. Occasionally, he was called on to interpret at the station, but not often. Jack held up two hands motioning for her to pause. She stopped signing and looked at him pointedly. She was still upset, but at least she had stopped screaming at him with her hands.

Jack once again held his fist to his chest, rotating it in a clockwise motion to say he was sorry. He also pulled out his badge and told her he was looking for a young auburn haired woman who had been in the bathroom. The deaf woman signed that she had seen a woman of Kelly's description leaving the restroom as she walked in. Jack inquired how long ago that was, and was informed it had been about ten minutes. Knowing she hadn't heard anything he let her go, thanking her by touching his chin with an upraised hand and lowering his hand to chest level.

Well that was certainly embarrassing, and not at all informative, Jack thought. He remembered the trash on the floor he was going to throw out and bent to retrieve it. The cloth felt slightly damp. Jack took a closer look at it. He saw a faint trace of smeared lipstick on the cloth. It was the same shade Kelly wore, light pink with a tinge of red. He lifted it to his nose and took a light sniff. That was when the smell of chloroform, mixed with lilacs, hit him full in the face.

The realization that this rag must have been pressed over Kelly's face was like a blow to his stomach. Jack's hands went to his gut, clutching the cloth tight; his body pausing while his mind whirled through the implications. Was Kelly right? Did they have the wrong guy? Was she in trouble? Was she already dead? Whoa! He stopped his thoughts right there. He refused to think that she might be beyond help. He couldn't go there right now. If he thought like that he would just collapse right here. No, Kelly had to be alive! Jack willed it with all his might.

Pushing down his thoughts, he focused on the facts. A rag with chloroform had been pressed to Kelly's mouth. No, not Kelly, think woman's mouth. Yes, impersonalize it. If he pretended it was just another missing person he might be able to function. If he could function he could help…the woman. Yes, he would concentrate on the clues at hand. Forget about what the monster had done whom had taken her. Forget who he had taken. "Just the facts Jack," he whispered to himself. Maybe it was another girl. Kelly fit the killer's profile though.

The rag was evidence. Jack carefully placed it in the pack, and searched the floor. There was one black mark that ran from the water fountain to a door nearby. It was like some-one had drug something across the floor; something fairly heavy on a solid piece of rubber. Jack bent over to touch the mark as if touching it would bring him closer to Kelly. The mark was indeed rubber. Jack pried a flake of it loose from the floor. Whatever it was, it was leaving a great trail. Jack followed the mark to a closed door. The dark grey color of the door was marred by a sign that said, "Authorized Person-nel Only!"

Drawing his gun, Jack stood to the side of the door, where the wall would help protect him from a bullet and slowly opened it. When there was no protest from inside he slammed it the rest of the way open and jumped inside. The hall light spilled inside and showed Jack a small concrete lined room.

Jack found the light switch and looked around. The room was about ten feet by eight feet and had some electrical equipment in it. There was also a black gate that was shut. This was an entrance to the steam tunnels. When he had first been a sophomore in college the University had closed the tunnels, even locking the gates. Why hadn't the room door been locked?

The university had constant problems with college kids in the tunnels for years. After they put on locks, Jack had not heard of any stray kids down in the tunnels. Jack knew he had never been able to get down there after they locked them. The school might never have locked them, except that they found asbestos in them. When they had to remove the asbestos they had to lock them down. Couldn't have some kid getting cancer, could they?

Jack supposed he should be grateful that they had locked the gates. He had been one of those kids after all. He loved to explore the tunnels. It was really great to run through them and play hide and go seek with the other kids. Jack would call his friends and they would all converge on the tunnels under his dormitory. They would take turns making up games to play; some of them not so innocent. Several times Jack had taken a willing girl to the dark tunnels to try to forget the pain of Kelly leaving him. He would smother himself in the strange girl's hair and dream Kelly while he released his tension. It was never good enough. Thoughts of Kelly stopped his day dreaming. He had to find her! He had to be her knight in shining armor.

Inspecting the gate from a distance didn't yield any clues. Jack moved closer carefully. The tunnel beyond was lit, but he knew they were hard to see down. There were lots of great hiding places and twists and turns. Steam pipes, wires and other utility things obstructed the lengths of tunnel that ran all under the campus. On closer inspection he could see that the gate's padlock had been popped.

Someone had carefully placed the padlock back into a locked position, but the mechanism was broken. Jack slipped the lock out of its hole. Gently, he pushed open the gate. The tunnels were well lit so he wouldn't need a flashlight. The problem would be in figuring out which way the guy had taken Kelly. The steam tunnels ran over the whole campus, carrying hot water for heat and electrical wires to the dorms and classrooms. He could only hope the kidnapper had left some clues for him to follow.

Jack had to think of it as a kidnapping. There was no blood on the floor, so he could hope that she was still alive. When he entered the tunnel additional marks joined the single black line. There were always two tracks through the dirt and grime on the concrete floor. Sometimes there were four, one of them always leaving a black streak. Now Jack was sure it was a wheeled cart with a heavy weight on it. The black line was bright, not dulled by dust. It was easy to follow. Jack traced the black line as far as it went. It wasn't far. The marks stopped at a door marked "High voltage, do not enter."

These signs had been enough to keep him out when he was a kid. He had seen way too many movies where the bad guy was done in by being too near a high voltage transformer. Even in his freshman year, in the depths of his despair over loosing Kelly, he had not been self-destructive. He had a healthy respect for electricity. Carefully, like he was afraid the door knob would bite him, he reached for the handle. It turned easily.

Jack entered the room, his drawn gun still leading the way. It was empty. The dirty floor had a smudge on it that could have been from a body. If it was, the body was long gone now. On one wall of the room there were four large levers, each labeled with a different building name. Jack inferred that this was the master control panel for the electricity to those buildings.

Not seeing anything of further help, Jack left the room. The drag mark ended here, along with any trace of Kelly or her kidnapper. Not having a better idea, Jack continued past the electrical room. He was starting to get more worried. Trying to move faster was proving difficult. His head was spinning with concern for Kelly and the tunnels were never meant to run through. There were lots of side tunnels and passages. Jack took time to look down each one, but he couldn't find any trace that someone had turned off the main branch. But he also couldn't find any trace that someone had passed the way he was traveling either.

The tunnel, seemed cleaner now, less dust on the floor. There was a breeze flowing through it, which probably helped keep the dust from settling on the floor. Jack was a tense bundle of nerves; a coiled spring ready to go off at any movement. There were no movements. The tunnels were deserted. He was completely alone.

Jack started to sweat. He was getting really hot. The air felt hotter also. Jack thought it was nerves; until he remembered the main heat plant for the campus. Tunnel rats nicknamed it The Dragon. There were more pipes, too, as the steam was routed to the rest of the campus. When he was a student the rumor was that some poor freshman had gotten drunk and fell down into the tunnels. He was too close to The Dragon and had died of dehydration. Jack recalled that the kids said it could reach one hundred fifteen degrees in here.

He must be getting close to The Dragon. It got so hot that Jack had to slow down. To continue he would have had to get on hands and knees. He sank to the floor in utter despair. Where was Kelly? How could he have yelled at her like he did? He loved her; loved her blindly. He would never forgive himself if she was killed. How could he go on? He had failed to back her up. She was in danger and it was as much his fault as the kidnapper's.

He had finally figured out he loved her and now she had been stolen from him. It wasn't fair. Jack gave in and sobbed. How could this happen to his wonderful Kelly? Knees pulled to his chest, head bowed, Jack looked like a broken man. Sweat from the heat ran in dirty streaks down his face. "Get it together, Jack," he whispered while pulling at his hair with both hands. "You have to get it together. This isn't helping Kelly," he said with more force. Showing an extreme amount of will power, Jack struggled to his feet. He staggered back the way he had come. Straightening more, determination crept into his steps.

He needed water and he needed more eyes on this case. In his haste and despair he had not called for backup. Now was the time to do that and widen the search. How big would this guy have to be to drag Kelly somewhere by himself? Once Kelly woke up she would fight him. Jack knew she was a fighter. The kidnapper would not be able to go fast with a struggling victim in tow. Jack had to think that Kelly was still alive. Since she was alive he knew she would aide his search. She would try everything in her power to leave him a trail of bread crumbs. If she was dead… he couldn't finish that thought. Jack couldn't believe she might be dead.

He retraced his steps. There had been a ladder leading to the surface a few side tunnels back. He stumbled toward it, breathing hard. The ladder was just where he remembered it. Scrambling up the rungs, he quickly reached the locked grate at the top. Now he would have to retrace his steps all the way back to the business school, half way across campus, before he could get out. Right back where I started, he thought, what a waste of time.

Jack was worried about what his boss would say when he reported this. How would he explain why Kelly ran off by herself?

There were strict guidelines when your partner started acting strange. If he didn't mention that he thought she was out of line earlier that evening, how would he explain her going off on her own? If he didn't blame her mental health, which would mean he had to bring up her misplaced guilt over Paul's death, then how did he explain her hair-brained loner act?

He was confused about what to say and how to say it, to keep everyone safe and yet get the help he needed. He would just have to wing it when the time came.

Jack finally traced his steps back to the gate with the broken lock. He walked through it and back into the building. The building was empty. It was also dark. Jack checked his watch. The luminous face showed 9:45. Now he was very concerned. Kelly had been missing for at least an hour now. His pulse raced. His stomach tied in knots from his anxiety. Every minute counted and he had wasted enough of them.

He turned to the water fountain first. After he slaked his thirst, he grabbed for his cell phone to report in and get some help. Excuses and plausible reasons danced on the tip of his tongue, but he didn't need them. His cell phone wasn't in his pocket.

Jack panicked for a moment thinking he had lost it in the tunnels until he remembered he had left it sitting on the counter in his kitchen. Now he wished he had just kept it in his pocket.

Nothing for it but to drive to the station. By the time he found a phone he could already be at the station. Besides, even though what Jack really wanted to do was to pound the pavement and wake up the whole campus trying to find Kelly, he knew that would be ineffective. The best use of his time would be to coordinate things from his office. From there he could keep appraised of what everyone found and when he heard the most likely lead he could chase it down.

He ran for his car. Climbing into the drivers' seat he was already outlining a plan before he even started the car. His captain would be off duty now, but he knew Captain Alice Boyd was usually in for the night shift. She would be sympathetic to his plight. She could definitely understand how Kelly might be feeling. It would add weight to his arguments about why she shouldn't be suspended for her actions, or him for his.

Jack pulled the small red flashing light out from behind the driver's seat. Reaching out his open window he slapped it onto the car roof. He heard the sharp ping as the light's magnet snapped it securely to the top of his car. Jack slapped the on switch and he had an emergency light. There was no siren in his personal car, and his handheld radio was at home, next to his phone. The department didn't even approve of lights in personal vehicles, but with Jack's record on the force, they looked the other way at this infraction.

He drove over the speed limit and cut a few yellow lights very close. Fortunately, he didn't have to run any red lights. The flashing red beacon on top of his car convinced most drivers to pull over. Jack always tried hard to set a good example with his driving, but tonight he would do what was necessary. Normally a ten minute drive, he made it to the station in five minutes flat. Surely, he could think of something to tell Alice that would keep him from getting fired while saving Kelly's life. Please Kelly, be alive.

Chapter Twelve

Jack's tires squealed in the parking garage as he slammed his car into a parking space. He hopped out, not bothering to lock it, and ran for the stairs. As he rounded the first landing, heading up, he almost ran over a fellow officer. Jack ignored the call of "What's the hurry Jack?" In truth he was so upset, tired and winded that he couldn't spare anything to even recognize the guy, much less apologize.

Jack paused at the top of the stairs to catch his breath and calm down for a minute before he went in to see the captain. It wouldn't do to burst into her office and not be able to say anything. He had to get forces mobilized in the shortest amount of time possible. The unusual long days, hard work out, and the running on campus coupled with the emotional strain of the last few hours, were about to catch up to him.

Captain Alice Boyd had her own office. Jack hardly ever had to walk past it. Now a distracted part of him noticed that the paint had been changed to chartreuse. Why on earth anyone would like that color of paint was beyond him. Alice's door was painted a hot pink. There was another one of those awkward motivational posters on her door.

The poster had a pink poodle on it. Half of the poodle had been shorn, and there was a hand in the photo ready to shear the other half. Just below the poodle's front paws the caption read, "There is no inevitability in history except as men make it. Felix Frankfurter." Jack spared only a second to register the sight of the pink poodle arguing with the bright door for dominance before he was inside and shutting the door behind him.

Alice sat behind her dark mahogany desk. Her office was cluttered with every kind of nick-knack in existence, most of it pink and revolving around cute little dogs. Jack ignored it all as he announced, "We have a problem."

"Just a moment, please." Alice dismissed the interruption.

"This is an emergency, Captain!" Jack was in no mood to wait.

"Okay, just a moment and I will be with you," she said in a voice that brooked no argument. Jack knew he would have to wait for a moment, if only to satisfy her ego. While he waited he mused on the poster. It had basically said for him to keep looking, keep striving to do better. Jack wanted to treat it like an omen, a good one, except he didn't buy into those kind of things. Who the heck was Felix Frankfurter anyway? He filed the name to look up later.

Taking a deep breath to interrupt, again, Alice forestalled him by looking up from her desk, "Jack! This is a surprise, what can I do for you?" She did a visible double take as she noticed his dirty, disheveled look, and added, "You look awful."

"I need to talk to you. We have a problem."

"Okay, I am all ears. How can I help?" Alice was curious.

"We have the wrong man behind bars. Well, actually, he should be behind bars, for assault of an officer, but not for the reason we thought." Jack stopped for a minute.

At the puzzled look on the captain's face he realized he wasn't making sense. Alice just sat there patiently looking at him. She was giving him all her attention. Jack slowed down and started again. "You know the guy we locked up for those murders?" She nodded and he continued, "He didn't kill those women. At least I don't think he did."

"Why not?" Captain Boyd wore a puzzled expression on her face. "Your report was very clear cut. You seemed to be very sure he did this morning. What has happened to change your mind? It isn't like you to second guess yourself, Jack."

"Kelly figured it out, but she is missing." Jack stumbled doggedly on.

"Missing? What happened?" Now Alice looked concerned.

"I think she was kidnapped by the murderer!"

"Okay, now you really have to stop and start again."

He was so overwhelmed and rushed that he felt like wringing his hands. Pacing would calm and order his thoughts, but there was no room. He had solved some tough cases while pacing. No way did Jack want to take this outside where others could hear what he had to say.

He took a deep breath he didn't feel he had time for, let it out and said, "Okay, the short version is that Kelly Swift, my new partner, figured out that there were too many holes in the case. She realized the guy we are holding, Frank, couldn't have committed the murders. I was very sure he had." Jack kicked himself, how could he have doubted her? "We had a big blow up about it. Anyway, by then it was too late. Kelly had a plan to act as bait to catch the guy. I didn't listen, but when what she said finally penetrated my thick skull, I realized I had to go after her." Jack would never forgive himself.

Oh, Kelly, where are you? Jack silently wondered. He was so worried about Kelly he couldn't think straight. His body was past the breaking point and running on shear willpower now. He would find her. He would save her. He would. He had to believe it. The other option was unthinkable.

Alice sat patiently while Jack visibly struggled to keep it together. He looked like a beaten man who didn't know it yet—dirty rumpled clothes, streaks of grime down his face, and a haunted look to his eyes. She wasn't sure how he kept on his feet. There was a chair in the room, but he showed no interest in sitting in it. Alice had noticed most of the men in the department stayed standing in her office. She had her suspicions that it had something to do with the neon pink chair sitting across from her desk. Jack took a deep breath which snapped her attention back to what he was saying.

"When I finally figured out where she had been, I tracked her. I found evidence that she was drugged with chloroform and hauled off. I searched for her until the trail went dead. I couldn't find her. We need to mobilize everyone. I can lead a party to try to find her," Jack said determinedly.

"No, Jack." Alice held up a hand to stop his protest. "I will order an APB on her. Someone will see her I'm sure. Also, I will send the forensics guys to where you found the evidence. They are capable of doing this without your inter-ference. Let them do their job. You will go home and get some sleep."

"No way, I can't go home! That is my partner out there," he insisted, slamming his fist on her desk for emphasis.

"Not only can you go home, but you will. It is after ten at night and your day starts at five tomorrow morning. You need to be fresh to try to put the clues together in the morn-ing. Without Kelly's help, it will all be on your shoulders. If you won't promise me that you will go home and get some rest I will send someone with you to make sure you do," Captain Boyd threatened.

Jack had to admit he was tired. He could hardly stay on his feet. He hadn't even eaten dinner. Maybe that was the problem. He should go home and grab a bite to eat, and after that he would feel better and could go help with the search. Not a chance he could sleep, not with Kelly in danger. Yes, that was a great plan.

"Okay, Captain, I will go home and have a bite to eat and try to sleep, but if I feel better after a nap I am back here and on the job. Deal?"

"I guess it will have to do. Now be sure to report what you found to forensics, and turn over any evidence to them, including location of the kidnapping," Alice said. "I'll call them and make sure they expedite this," she finished, match-ing action to words and picking up the phone.

Jack took this as a dismissal. He was on the way out the door when she covered the mouth piece of the phone and called out, "Oh, and Jack, the senior detective's job is to en-sure that rookies know how the department works and keep them out of trouble. I don't think you did a very good job of keeping track of Kelly Swift or her wild schemes. Your experience is supposed to temper hers. I have no idea what you were thinking letting her go off halfcocked like that. We will talk, with your captain, about this later."

"Yes, ma'am," Jack replied dejectedly.

Chapter Thirteen

Kelly woke with a headache, having no idea of where she was. Her head was fuzzy, and her hands tied together. Her feet felt like they were made of lead bricks. Her thoughts spun in circles, but the one thing that kept shooting through her mind was that she had really done it now. She was in big time trouble—trouble she wasn't at all sure she could get out of.

It was dark. Trying to sit up she hit her head on something. Kelly blinked a few times. She squeezed her eyes shut tight and opened them wide. She still couldn't see. Even with her eyes open she saw flashes of blue and red like fireworks in her mind. She recognized the effects of opening your eyes in total darkness. Between mostly numb hands and the pitch blackness she was starting to lose it. Her heart raced and her breathing started speeding up. The sensory deprivation was threatening to overwhelm her. She knew she had to get a grip on herself. She might cause more damage to her body if she didn't calm down.

Fighting off panic, Kelly concentrated on her breathing. She took long slow breaths, counting slowly each time. One, two, three, four, five for the inhale and one, two, three, four, five, six for the exhale. Kelly had practiced Yoga since high school, long before it became fashionable again. She knew how centering and calming it could be to just breathe. Inhale one, two three, four, five. Panicking doesn't help. Exhale, one. Two. Three. Four. Five. Six.

A few dark shadows began to take shape, so it wasn't totally dark after all. At least she wasn't blind, one less thing to freak about. Inhale, one. Two. Three. Four. Five. Calm down and think. Exhale, one. Two. Three. Four. Five. Six.

Kelly wiggled her fingers painfully, one by one. Next she spread all her fingers out to as far as they would go. She concentrated on getting her thumbs to open wide. Inhale one, two three, four, five. You can do this. Exhale, one. Two. Three. Four. Five. Six. Next she moved her toes, pointing them out like a Barbie doll's feet. She flexed the toes and finally she spread them like she had her fingers. Inhale one, two three, four, five. You will find a way to escape. Exhale, one. Two. Three. Four. Five. Six.

It only took two or three minutes to go through these basic stretches. After the first minute, the panic had receded a bit and by the end Kelly was somewhat centered and ready to think. She let her breathing go back to normal and concentrated on trying to remember what had happened.

It was then that she remembered the day. She remembered her argument with Jack. A sharp stab of pain hit her like a physical blow to the chest. Jack hated her. The feeling was intense. Kelly brought her bound hands to her chest. She gasped when needles stabbed her wrists as circulation tried to come back; all of her careful breathing forgotten with the pain of remembering him.

He had dismissed her from his bed. He couldn't handle being with her after she had admitted to getting Paul killed. She couldn't blame him. She knew it would come to that. She constantly battled with her own self-loathing over the same issue. Foolishly she had hoped Jack would still love her enough to forgive her. It was an impractical hope. How could he absolve her when she couldn't pardon herself? Despair threatened to overwhelm her.

Kelly felt little reason to keep on living. She had never expected to be so head over heels in love with Jack. Some part of her must have known that it wasn't just puppy love. His rebuff was devastating. Kelly curled into herself fighting the emotional pain. She stretched her fingers again in an attempt to distract herself and took a few careful breaths. She felt like she might explode any minute.

By sheer force of will alone she turned her thoughts away from Jack and to her situation. It had happened so fast. How had she been taken by surprise? The hall had been empty, and then…it wasn't. Everything had seemed to happen at once. She had wanted Jack there as backup. She had assumed he could wait outside in the car, ready to tail them if the murderer took her. Even if Jack had been there, he could never have gotten to her in time. A little voice in her head whispered, 'exactly! You couldn't help Paul either,' but Kelly pushed it away, hard. There could be no forgiveness for her cowardliness.

Kelly tested her confines, more slowly this time. Above her a metal surface refused to give when she pushed on it. Kelly rolled to her left side and stretched out her hands. It felt like carpet under them, but she couldn't feel a wall to her room. The carpet wasn't thick. It was very rough and not at all plush. It was like a business building's carpet. The numbness in her hands didn't help her distinguish anything either. She wanted to know the extent of the room she was in. How big was it?

Instead of wiggling her whole body over she reached out with her feet. Her bare toes hit the cold hard metal wall beside her. Where were her shoes? How had she lost them? The panic started to overwhelm her again, making her little box seem even smaller than it was. Eventually she remembered taking them off before going out into the hall.

That had been really stupid. She had just assumed that the kidnapping would happen after class. She never thought anyone would try anything with that many people around. Of course, she reflected, there hadn't been anyone around in the hallway.

With great difficulty Kelly stopped hyperventilating and calmed the runaway thoughts flying through her mind. She hated losing control and she despised the weakness that her claustrophobia left her feeling. Anytime she was in a small place it became very difficult to think. Her limbs would grow weak and the panic would try to push its way through the walls in her mind. She had to fight the feeling with all her might. The darkness made her react the same way the claustrophobia did. The two together left her fighting for her sanity.

Another deep calming breath. She had to keep thinking. She had to keep trying to get more control. Control was the only thing that would help that tight anxious feeling in her chest. Kelly forced herself back to some action. Anything to keep doing something, she thought. Time to check to the right. She wiggled and squirmed until she finally made it to her right side. She reached out with her hands, slowly. After a few inches she met resistance. Instead of hard metal she felt something slightly giving. Her bound hands explored until she felt hair under her fingers. Her hands jerked back to her chest in surprise. She tried whispering, "Hey, you okay?" It came out as a croak. Swallowing she tried again. This time it was louder, but still quiet enough Kelly hoped it wouldn't be heard outside her cage. Kelly didn't want to draw the kidnapper's attention.

There was no response. More than that it was absolutely silent. Kelly knew it was wrong for it to be so quiet, but she couldn't focus on it. She was using most of her brain just to endure the stifling environment.

She tentatively reached out for the person again. She found the hair, long and soft. A girl or woman, she thought. Following the hair to the woman's shoulder she pushed on her shoulder gently. Kelly had no idea if the woman was hurt or not, so she was being very careful. The shoulder didn't feel quite right. It was too firm, not real enough. Kelly had a bad feeling about this. The silence intruded on her thoughts again. Kelly held her breath and listened for the other woman to breath. Kelly didn't hear anything. Kelly's breathing started to get faster again. She truly hoped she was wrong. Please, don't let there be a dead body in here with me, she silently begged.

Further groping with her hands confirmed it was without a doubt a dead body. The chest didn't move, but there were breasts, so it was a woman. The body wasn't even warm and it was very stiff. Kelly crept, on her side, away from the body till she hit her back on the wall. Kelly curled into a fetal position, to keep warm, and think. Kelly locked the part of her brain away that was gibbering at her to run. She would not panic again. She was strong and had a lot of training. She could get out of this. She had to; there was no help in sight.

Jack headed from the station to his car after handing off the cloth to forensics. He was still berating himself for letting Kelly go off on her own. His mind wouldn't leave it alone even for the short drive home. How could he? What had he been thinking? He had just had the most wonderful sex of his life, even better than that night ten years ago. Then he had blown up at the only woman he had ever loved. Now she was missing and he might never get to say he was sorry.

Jack knew he had acted childishly. Kelly had trusted him with her fears as well as with her theory. He had pushed it all aside. He had ignored her. Even if he did find her she would probably never forgive him. He had to find her. Maybe if he rode to the rescue she would at least listen to his apology before kicking him out of her life for good. Maybe she would have pity on him. He had to find her before he could find a way to tell her he loved her.

His house came into view down the street. The lights were still on in the living room, reminding him of where the night had started. He couldn't believe what a demanding tiger she had been in bed. He could still feel her skin against his if he held still. Such an intense longing pierced his gut that he almost drove past the house and on toward campus. He really wanted to help lead the search and make sure no one missed anything.

They needed to find every single clue. He needed to find Kelly. The forensics people were good. Night shift or day they were all competent, more than competent. They were the best in the state. Jack had to admit they could do their job better if he wasn't hanging around in the way. They could tell him everything they found after his nap. Forensics was a science and science took time. Jack had heard Sue say it so many times he actually heard her voice when he thought about that rule.

He would get something to eat before he would go ask them what they found. He would make sure they understood where he had gone, what he had deduced and where he thought they should look from there. He pulled into his driveway and stumbled into his house. The problem with being in really good shape was the need to consume lots of calories during the day. No fat reserves to carry you through. Jack was fighting a crash brought on by lack of fuel. His body was a finely tuned machine and not used to going without nourishment.

Jack stumbled into his kitchen. He was working on automatic at this point. He opened the refrigerator and just stared into it. He didn't really care what he ate. He reached in and pulled out the makings for a sandwich.

Lathering a piece of bread with mustard, then layering it with left over fresh baked chicken breast, Jack started a hasty sandwich. Sliced tomatoes came next, followed by another piece of bread. He was too tired to get out all the fixings so this would have to do. Pouring a large glass of milk, he set the meal on a tray and carried it to the living room to eat on the couch. The food was consumed mechanically. He didn't think he would sleep, but the next thing he knew he was dreaming.

Kelly thought furiously. The murderer had fallen for the trick. He had taken the bait. She should have been elated, except, unfortunately, she was the bait. She clearly had no idea where she was. Jack wouldn't even notice her missing until morning and it would be too late. Her brain was getting less foggy now.

She could remember someone holding a cloth over her nose. Vaguely remembered waking up on a cart that was rolling through a short concrete tunnel; no, not just a short tunnel, a long underground tunnel. The lights seemed to flicker as she was rolled past pipes and strange looking wires. She remembered trying to pay attention, trying to leave traces behind. She couldn't remember if she had succeeded. She must have passed out again. The next time she woke had been in this cage. Wishing to be home safe in bed, she instead found she was getting cold, and had no idea where she was.

Kelly dosed off, thinking about how much better this would have been if she had never told Jack about Paul. She might have had backup or she might even still be in Jack's bed. Closing her eyes, she could feel Jack's strong arms tight around her. She curled into a tight ball to keep her warm and for the comfort of it. A noise startled her back into awareness. A key was turning in a lock. Kelly tried to move a little, but she was too stiff from the cramped position she had been in. It must have been several hours since she had first woken.

Chapter Fourteen

The darkness lifted suddenly, along with the metal roof above her head. Kelly blinked a couple of times in the bright light, her stressed brain finally grasping that she was trapped in a car trunk. Panic threatened again as she realized she could be anywhere. She might never be found. There was a man looking down at her.

He appeared to be about 45. A receding hairline and bad comb-over job did nothing to help his appearance. He was rough looking, raw around the edges. His eyes open wide, frantic. The look someone gets when backed into a corner by a wild bear with no choice but to shoot or be eaten. Kelly would not have been surprised to see foam at his mouth. She looked for it, but what she saw was raw determination in the set of his lips. Naturally thin, they were like two narrow straight lines pinched together.

Spittle accompanied the words as he spoke. "Ah, I thought you would be awake. Too bad I can't say the same thing for your friend over there." He laughed a little, a mad, insane laugh.

He leaned in and Kelly cringed away from him. He laughed again, bending in further to hoist Kelly up and out of the trunk of his car. She gagged a little at the smell of him, the stench of days' old sweat and stress wafting off him.

The man roughly stood her on her feet. His hands on her arms were insistent and firm, but the grip didn't hurt. Kelly was careful to take her time, muscles complaining about the abuse they had taken. It was painful to straighten after all that time curled up, but she also moved slowly to assess the man, looking for any weaknesses.

Kelly didn't see a gun, but that didn't mean there wasn't one. As she stepped to the ground she took a deep breath and let her body sag, suddenly. The man was able to catch her weight and keep her upright. So he was stronger than he appeared. He was also a few inches taller than her. Most of his height seemed to be in his legs, so she probably couldn't outrun him, particularly with bound hands.

Her only option would be to disable him. The thought sent a chill up her spine. The academy taught hand to hand combat training, but she never expected to use it. After all they were issued guns for a reason. In fact, they received much more time on the gun range than they did on the Karate mats.

Kelly took a look around. She was at a park that she didn't recognize at first. He had parked the car in a spot next to a handicapped spot. Kelly noted, inanely, that some part of him must be a law abiding citizen. He was definitely messed up in the head if he bothered to obey the handicapped law, but still killed people.

The park had a stream running nearby. Kelly shifted her feet a little, trying to get the sharp points of the gravel out from under them. She liked to go barefoot and that probably helped her now, but she didn't usually go barefoot over rough gravel. Her wiggling only managed to put the sharp point away from her toes and under her instep. The pointed pain made her wiggle more than she wanted to. She gritted her teeth together tightly to keep any sound from emerging.

The man interrupted her squirming with a little shake. "What is your name, pretty lady?" He asked, his words drawled out with a southern accent.

Kelly thought about not answering, but she decided that she could give him her first name. There was no sense in letting him know she would be stubborn. Maybe if she played along she could lull him into believing she wouldn't give him any trouble. The more she got him to relax the better her chances of escaping.

"Kelly," she offered with a shaky voice she didn't have to fake.

"Hi, Kelly, I'm Albert. I wish I could have met you under different circumstances." With a little laugh he continued, "You just wait right there while I take care of this poor excuse for a woman."

When Albert turned his back on Kelly she figured it was her chance. Ignoring the cold, sharp pebbles biting into her feet she lurched forward. Albert must have been expecting something because he neatly sidestepped her. Her momentum carried her into the unforgiving edge of the trunk. Kelly doubled over and her face landed on the dead body in the trunk. All the air rushed out of her lungs in one big gasp.

"See, now why did you have to go and do that?" Albert drawled. "I don't want to kill you today, I have plans for you." He set a heavy hand on her shoulder. She was afraid for a minute he was going to shove her in the trunk, or smash her head in with the lid. The heavy hand grabbed part of her jacket and hauled back on it. Kelly had no choice but to straighten up. She pushed a little with her bound hands to help keep her jacket from ripping.

For a minute Kelly panicked as he pulled her back upright. She did not want to end up strung in a tree and shot. She just about gave in to hysteria at the thought of Jack finding her desecrated corpse like that. "No, please," she begged. "I promise I won't do it again."

"No, you won't because you won't have another chance," Albert said. He pulled a coarse rough rope out of the car. It was the same kind of rope he had tied up the first four women with. Kelly really was panicked now. She was about to be one of the next two victims.

Kelly wanted to run. All her instincts told her to flee. Every ounce of her self-control was needed to calm down and concentrate. What could she do to convince him to spare her life? Begging obviously hadn't worked, but what else was there? She closed her eyes while she thought. She couldn't win by brute strength. Maybe threatening would do it. If she could bluff her way out of this...

Kelly looked him straight in the eye and mustered all her courage to say, "I am a Boulder Police Detective. My partner will be here any minute to find me." She paused to emphasize the seriousness of the situation to him. "He will catch you. If you kill me he will never let you stand trial. He will kill you. If you let me go I can walk back to town and give you time to get away." The last was added as a bribe. Kelly had no intention of letting him get away.

"Oh, and you would let me go just like that, would you?" Albert asked sarcastically. Shoving her onto the ground and tying her ankles together, Albert said, "I already knew that. I saw your picture on the front of the morning newspaper. You know they have it all wrong." At this he laughed adding, "I have you all fooled."

"Why don't you tell me how you did it? Where did we go wrong?" Kelly stalled for more time to think.

Albert pulled her over the rough ground to a nearby picnic table. The rocks cut into her butt and calves. Here he cut the ropes binding her hands and roughly pulled them behind her. He bound them again. He really wasn't taking any chances with her. Next he wrapped ropes tightly around her chest. After she was trussed up like a pig at a boar bake, he fed the ropes around a picnic table to make sure she stayed in place. The whole time he worked at the ropes he kept up a litany of why he had taken her.

"You think you are so smart. I will give it to you that you figured out where I was finding these traitors, but you didn't think to protect yourself. It was so easy to grab you. I can't believe you even figured out where the women were coming from. But, I know I still have the upper hand because I have you. The department will be going crazy searching for you, but they will be too late."

Kelly kept trying to think of a way out. She was completely convinced he would kill her. He really had nothing to lose and she had nothing to convince him to keep her alive.

Her one consolation was that he said he wasn't going to kill her today. Albert finished the last knot and made sure it was secure. Kelly wasn't sure why he thought it was necessary to tie her to the table.

"No time to talk, right now. I have a murder to stage." He must have seen the fear in her eyes because he added, "No, not yours, my dear. Hers," he said, pointing at the body in the trunk. "Your death can wait a day or two. Keep me company. I am curious about why you would put yourself in harm's way. What did you think you would accomplish?"

This last was said like he didn't really want an answer. Having secured her tightly enough she couldn't take a deep breath, he was already bent back over trying to lift the dead weight out of his trunk. Albert succeeded and Kelly kept quiet while he secured the poor woman to a tree.

The part of Kelly that was a detective watched with detached curiosity. Here the crime was being laid out before her. She would not have to wonder about his methodology, she would know how he did it. If she could escape, that knowledge might save more women. She was determined to find a way to escape.

Albert had given her hope when he said she wouldn't be killed immediately. Even tied to the bench, straining to breathe, she was able to find hope. She also noticed her numb fingers were touching the ground. A small plan started to take hold in her mind.

Albert threw a long length of rope over a high branch. He secured one end to the victim's tied hands. Taking the other end in his hands he hoisted the body into the tree. It did not look to be easy for him and it took him a long time. Kelly was thankful for the extra time.

Her fingers hurt from scratching in the dirt. She had no idea if what she was trying was going to work. Would Jack or the forensics team even find it? She almost gave up more than once. When her fingers throbbed too much for her to go on she rested them and flexed them.

Kelly briefly entertained the idea of screaming, but she didn't want to draw Albert's attention to herself. The body didn't care what Albert did to it now, but Kelly certainly did. Kelly also was aware of her oath to protect and serve. If she called out and someone came to her rescue, the person might get shot.

She had wondered why the women hadn't screamed at the other two murder scenes. Now she knew. They were already dead. That was why no one heard a struggle. Kelly was very sure that all the women had been killed before being taken to the parks where they had been found. She wasn't sure about the blood they had found, because a dead body doesn't bleed when shot. Her fingers kept scratching as she distracted herself from the pain; her brain chewing on the problem of the case.

She didn't have to wonder long. Albert lined up the body facing out into the woods, like the others had been. He pulled out a large caliber pistol and put a silencer on it. So, mystery two solved. Albert placed a single shot through the dead woman's head. Kelly had to wonder why he bothered. He walked back over to the car. Opening the back door he hauled out a red bag. As he walked back by her, she could see it was a pint of blood, like one from a blood bank. She couldn't quite make out the label on the bag, but she recognized the style of bag.

Back at the body, Albert opened the bag with a sharp knife. He held the small slit high over his head. Carefully, like he had all the time in the world, he poured the blood down the chin of the body and down the chest, till it pooled on the ground. Now she knew how he had staged the murder and why forensics had been fooled for a while. By now forensics probably had a more accurate picture of what had really happened. Too bad it was too late to help the woman hanging in the tree.

Kelly reflected that it might be too late to help her too. Albert cleaned up after himself, checking around carefully to make sure he hadn't missed anything. Stepping back to take one last look at the woman in the tree, he dropped to his knees. Kelly thought he was crying at first, but she saw he was praying. Kelly wondered at this. Maybe she would get a chance to ask him later. What would lead a man to take women's lives and pray about it? Kelly hoped she lived to find out.

Albert walked back over to her and said, "You can sit in the car with me if you behave."

Kelly just nodded, not trusting herself to speak. She knew any promise she made to this monster wasn't binding, but she didn't want to give her word. She needed to be able to take advantage of any chance to escape. Kelly knew herself well enough to know that if she gave her parole it might keep her from acting when she needed to.

Albert cut loose the ropes binding her to the table leg. She took deep grateful breaths, wishing she could rub her chest where the ropes had bit into her. Next he cut the ropes holding her feet. This time Kelly instantly got to her feet and sedately followed him to the car, she didn't want Albert to notice the marks on the ground behind where she had been sitting.

At the car, Albert wasn't dumb enough to put her in the back seat. In fact, Kelly didn't think he was dumb at all. Disturbed? Yes. Dumb? No. Too bad. It would make escaping all the tougher.

Albert eased her into the passenger seat in the front of the car. He took out his knife, and, pushing her forward, cut the bonds around her wrists. Kelly brought her hands in front of her and rubbed at her wrists, noticing that her fingers were in sad shape. Quickly, hoping Albert hadn't noticed the dirt and bloody cracks, Kelly closed her hands into fists. Albert expertly tied her hands together in front of her.

Sedately, Albert pulled out of the parking lot and onto the highway heading up Boulder Canyon. Kelly was going crazy. The sky was getting lighter, yet it would be a few hours before the sun kissed the floor of the canyon. Still, she hoped, and dreaded, that someone would pull into the parking lot and see them.

She hoped so because it might help Jack find her and she dreaded it because, until Albert drove off, anyone seeing him might be in danger. The suspense was too much and she had to calm herself by looking out the window at the canyon as they drove.

Rocks rushed past her, just a few feet off the road. There were not many trees in this stretch of the canyon; the walls were just too steep to allow vegetation. As they climbed the canyon it opened out a bit more. A few bushes and trees lined the edge of the road. Kelly knew there were more on the other side of the road, next to the river, but she didn't want to look that way and risk catching Albert's eye.

A half hour later saw them pulling up a little used side road. The road quickly turned to dirt and Albert slowed down. Kelly had been keeping track of all the twists and turns. The road climbed steeply and soon they passed a chain link fence. The fence ran almost a half mile down the road before curving away from them and running farther than she could see. She idly wondered what it was for.

Kelly had not dared to make conversation, not wanting to draw his attention. Instead she used the time to think about her escape. When that didn't produce very many options, she turned her thoughts back to her situation and to Jack. She could still dream about Jack, even if he didn't want her anymore. Dreaming was more pleasant than reality.

When she closed her eyes, memories of yesterday floated in her mind like a sun-filled day, warm, happy and relaxed. Jack's arms had been so affectionate, his touch so sure, she just wanted to lie in them forever. If she had not been in so much discomfort she was sure her body would have reacted to the memories. As it was she still blushed to think about how slowly he tried to take it. She knew he would have given her as much attention as she could handle, and regretted having rushed him.

When the dirt road changed to more path than road, Albert pulled over to the side and stopped. Kelly snapped out of her daydream. She sat up quickly, realizing he could have taken several turns after he left the road and she wouldn't have known it. She silently cursed her daydreaming and her hormones. This was no time to be thinking about the impossible to catch, perfect man. If nothing else, she needed an impossible escape first.

Chapter Fifteen

Jack woke from a nightmare. Kelly was dead and hanging in a tree. For a minute he was unsure if he had been dreaming, or if it had been real. Taking stock of where he was, he concluded that it had been a dream and relaxed. He took a longer look around, trying to wake all the way up.

Miraculously, his glass of milk remained right side up. The sandwich had not been so lucky; about half of it was on the floor. Jack groaned as he sat up. His back hurt from sleeping on the couch. Quickly checking his watch, he remembered that Kelly had been kidnapped. It read 5:00 am. He was already late for his morning ritual. The five or six hours of sleep left him more alert even if it didn't leave him feeling very rested.

He rubbed his hands down his face, bouncing a little to get to the edge of the couch, not quite ready to stand up yet. Finally, gingerly, he stood and headed to the bathroom. He was waking up fast now. It was all coming back to him. He had to get a move on. Brushing his teeth and relieving himself were the priority. Coming out of the bathroom, still wiping the extra water off his face, his phone rang. He answered it on the third ring, "Hello, Detective Hall."

"Jack, you awake?" Jack recognized his captain's voice. The captain continued without waiting for a reply. "Another body was reported, at Centennial Park, out on the west edge of town, can you meet the team there?"

Jack didn't even hear the last question; he slammed the receiver down and was already running for his car.

Pulling into the parking lot at Centennial, Jack opened his car door even before he turned it off. He was out and running for the police tape instantly. The sight of a woman with auburn hair, arms tied above her head, hanging in a tree jerked him up short. Breath catching in his throat, Jack ducked under the police tape more slowly. If it was Kelly he didn't want to know. He didn't see how it could be anyone else. The kidnapper had broken from his MO, the tree held only one body. Kelly would appreciate that. At least one woman had been spared.

Jack averted his glaze. He didn't want to confirm his worst nightmare. He didn't want to know that he had let his partner, lover, and only love, down. He would never forgive himself. Life would not be worth living without Kelly in it. Jack knew the world would hold no joy for him without her; he would not rest until he found her killer.

With this final thought firmly in mind he looked up at the woman in the tree. Immediately he realized it couldn't have been Kelly. The woman in the tree had her same hair and eyes, but she had to be about 3 inches taller than Kelly.

The giddy feeling in his chest was suddenly replaced by a sense of guilt. He had no right to be happy. A woman was still dead. This poor woman was important to someone. Jack might be relieved, but somewhere someone was going to get a call and his life would stop. Still his urge to give a little whoop of joy was hard to suppress. Kelly was alive! He still had a chance to ask her forgiveness.

His immediate fears absolved, Jack was able to revert back to detective mode. His chest tightened and his head spun. Kelly had been right. Frank was not the serial murderer. He realized he had not totally believed her theory until that moment. He wasn't sure what he had believed. Maybe he had held out hope that it was a random kidnapping and that she would be returned safe.

What he had thought didn't matter now. With a physical effort he pulled his thoughts back to the task at hand. He had to concentrate. Jack looked around. He was both elated that the killer had varied from his M.O. and also scared. Why didn't the murderer kill Kelly too? How much time did she have? How was Jack going to find this fiend?

One thing was sure at this point, Jack needed more clues. He needed to get busy. This park didn't have any houses nearby so that would save him time. He wouldn't have to ask meaningless questions of people who didn't know anything. In fact, now that Jack looked around he noticed that there was not a single spectator here. Centennial Park was farther out from the center of the town so Jack guessed it would not get the early morning hikers. This begged the question of who called it in.

Jack would find that out back at headquarters. He took a good look around. The scene was the same as last time, but there was only one body. Thank goodness it wasn't Kelly! Jack spotted Doug, the coroner, walking toward him. "Hi, Jack. I heard about Kelly. I'm sorry."

Jack managed, "Thank you. Now find me a clue that will lead to this guy. I want him bad and I want Kelly back!"

Having said this Jack turned on his heel and walked purposely back to his car. He drove carefully back to the station. Kelly was still alive. It was like a mantra in his head. Kelly was alive. It gave Jack hope, where he had not had any before. He had to find her. Jack had a nagging feeling that he was out of time. Some inner alarm was going off saying that he had to hurry, had to find her before the next morning. He always trusted his feelings. He certainly wasn't going to ignore this one.

In his office, Jack pulled out his notes on the case. Not much to go on. He made some additional notes at the bottom of the sheet. They were simple. Where? Who? How? When? He sat back to ponder these questions. The 'where' applied both to, "Where was the guy holding Kelly?" and, "Where would the next murder happen?" If he couldn't figure out the first, puzzling out the second would at least give him a chance to get there before Kelly was killed. Jack could stop the murderer at the next park, before Kelly was killed.

Jack pulled out a map of Boulder County. Marking all three parks where the murders had happened with a red dot. After that he sat back and just stared at the map. Not seeing any obvious pattern his head drifted. When he found Kelly the first thing he would do was apologize. He would sweep her into his arms and not set her down for a week. Finally. he would ask her to marry him and wouldn't take no for an answer. As he daydreamed about the wedding his subconscious brain worked on the problem of the map.

Suddenly, Jack bolted upright in his seat; he knew where the next park would be. Or rather what kind of park it would have to be. The parks all had several commonalities. Each of their names started with a 'C' and each one led further into the Rocky Mountains. They all had lots of tree coverage and were slightly secluded, but not so far removed that people wouldn't stumble on the bodies. Now he just had to find it on his maps.

Scanning his map of Boulder County he couldn't find another park that started with 'C'. Frustrated he switched to his state map of the roads and recreational parks in Colorado. Following a hunch he traced Highway 119 out of Boulder, west, toward Nederland. There in the south side of Nederland was a park. Looking closely, Jack saw the name. His heart skipped a beat – Chipeta Park – was written in tiny black letters on the small space of green.

Jack couldn't remember going there himself, but it looked big enough to have hiking trails. Nestled in the mountains it would have places to fit the serial murders M.O. Chipeta Park had to be the next location. He could feel it in his gut. That was where the next murder would be.

The when was easy, it would be tomorrow morning, early. Jack wasn't sure if there would be one or two bodies, but he didn't want to wait to find out. The who... that didn't really matter right now. If they met the murderer at the park, they would find out who.

It was like the guy was taunting Jack. Teasing him. Daring Jack to catch him. Jack wasn't happy just knowing where the next murder would take place or even when, preferring to find Kelly today. Now. Before she could be hurt. When he caught this guy he would make sure he didn't get away.

Jack pushed back his chair with a sigh. Standing, he stretched his aching back. With purposeful strides he headed for forensics. They had better be able to tell him more now. It had been two full days since the first murder and no one could hide all their tracks.

Albert opened Kelly's door. When she put her feet down outside the car it was to step into two inches of snow. Kelly was very cold by the time Albert led her, still barefoot, into his cabin. Kelly was looking forward to being in the warm cabin. However, when she stepped inside, she discovered it was colder than outside. Her teeth started to chatter. Albert, hearing them, said, "Don't worry, tomorrow or the next day you'll be hot enough…in Hell."

"Please just let me go. By the time I find my way out of here I'll be so lost I couldn't lead them back here if I wanted to. Please just let me go," Kelly begged.

"No chance, pretty thing. If I let you go…well it would just be bad. Nope, it wouldn't be good for you, or for me." Albert shook his head. He busied himself putting wood in the potbellied stove in the middle of the cabin. "Have a seat," he instructed.

Kelly looked around the cabin. She saw only one chair. It was large and cushy looking. She started toward it, but Albert interrupted her, "No! That chair is mine." Kelly stood there for a moment, lost. Not seeing an alternative, she sat on the floor. The rough cut lumber was worn smooth from years of use. Once seated, Kelly took a long moment to look around.

The walls were all paneling on the inside with tongue and groove planks in the ceiling. A reddish color made the wood look like cherry, but the grain was all pine. To the left of the only door was a small kitchen. It looked spotless. In fact the whole place looked well-kept and homey. It really didn't fit with what she had seen of Albert's personality.

There was a bed in one corner. No way was she going to share it with Albert. She would fight tooth and nail before she would let that happen.

She heard him laugh and turned. He was staring at her. Albert had noticed where she was looking and seen her shudder. Maybe he didn't intend to wait until night. "Not to worry," Albert said, relieving one of her fears, "I have no intention of having sex with you. I will roll out a bedroll tonight and you can sleep in it. I will of course be tying you up, so you might as well forget trying to get out of here."

Kelly sat on the floor and stared out the one big window at the valley far below. Even if she did escape, she didn't have much chance of reaching help before she froze to death. She might have to wait until she could get his car keys. It was looking bleaker and bleaker as the sun rose higher in the sky, finally kissing the valley floor with its light.

Jack strode into forensics, "What do you guys have for me?"

"I was just on my way to get you. The night team found something that might help you, but first I have a synopsis from our analysis of the first two murder scenes," Susan said.

"Okay, I'm all ears."

"Well, to start with the women were not killed by the bullet." She held up a forestalling hand to ward off his obvious questions. Jack obligingly clamped his lips shut over what he had been about to say and gave her his full attention. Sue continued, "They were already dead." Jack's heart stopped. He paled as Sue finished, "The blood looked fresh because it had anti-coagulant in it. It was blood from a blood bank."

Jack's puzzled look was slowly turning to one of understanding, "So, the women were already dead before they were hung from the tree?" At Sue's nod Jack continued, "and the whole thing, the blood and bound hands were to throw us off? So when were they killed?"

Sue knew Jack wouldn't like the next answer, "Jack, they were dead over 24 hours before they were hung in the tree and desecrated."

No! Jack almost flew into a panic. It meant that he couldn't just wait to meet them at Chipeta Park. His Kelly could be dead and just not on display yet. His beautiful Kelly, whom he was determined to marry. Jack couldn't think about it. For about the hundredth time since the kidnapping, Jack pushed that thought to the back of his mind, erecting walls around the thought so it couldn't escape to torment him. He put up a picture of Kelly in his mind's eye. Her perfect curves, her soft hips, her tasty lips. He would hold onto this image to keep him sane until he found her. I'm coming for you my love! Hang on!

"Kelly is still alive!" Jack snapped at Sue with more violence than he meant to. At her startled look he quickly apologized. "Sorry, Sue, this isn't your fault. Did you get anything more from the murder scenes?"

"Yesterday's murder scene was like the first, but we got three things more. One from the latest murder scene, and two from the business school where Kelly was taken."

"Don't keep me waiting!"

Sue calmly continued, "Well, in the school we found a few boot prints. The boots had a funny wear pattern on the outside of the right leg, which implies a limp on that side. That was number one. Number two was dirt found in the boot print. It was strange red clay. This in itself was not that significant, but when you consider you have to dig down a ways or go wading in the river that runs down the Boulder Canyon, well…"

"Great! This means our guy probably walked in the creek down the Boulder Canyon. There is only 30 miles of creek!" Jack said sarcastically. "I'll start walking right now."

"Sorry, Jack, I'll cut to the chase. This clay is only found in the section of the river that the falls are on. So in other words, the clay gets washed down to the river in the valley from the mountains. It only pools in the pond below the waterfall. Unless our guy was wading there, which I highly doubt as it is 40 feet deep, he could only have gotten the clay from the old Sign Mine site. It is the only other place that exact clay is found. If I was guessing I would say he is holed up near there, or at least keeping his victims there."

"Thanks," Jack called turning to head out of the office.

"Uh, Jack, one more thing." Jack turned back. He was anxious to get going.

"There was evidence that someone was tied to the picnic table at the Creekside Park. Someone, presumably Kelly, scratched a name into the dirt. We also found fragments from the rope tied around the victims' hands near the table. We think he had Kelly tied up to the table while he set the last scene up for us to find. The name was 'Albert.' Sorry, I know it isn't much to go on. Good luck!"

Now Jack really was out of there like a flash. He actually ran to his office. He needed to grab a couple of things and make a few phone calls before he could put his rapidly-forming plan into action. Now that he knew he couldn't just wait for morning to rescue Kelly, he was determined to get there as soon as possible. All he had to do was put the clues together to figure out where there was. He hated the thought of Kelly in a cold dark mine, scared, lonely, and thinking he hated her. Jack was determined to ride to her rescue, like a knight in shining armor. Hang on Kelly!

Chapter Sixteen

Kelly's teeth no longer chattered; the cabin was warming up. Albert pulled a folding chair from some unseen corner and helped her up into it. He didn't offer her a blanket or the slippers, which would have helped. It was very difficult to think about escaping when your feet were cold and bare. Dress shoes wouldn't have been much better, but they would have made her feel less vulnerable.

She knew it would be dangerous to leave the cabin, unless she could do it before dark. Her jacket wasn't very warm. Yesterday, in town, it had been a crisp sixty out and today it had felt more like forty. At this altitude it would be even colder; she could freeze to death before she could make her way back down to the road.

Albert loosened the bonds on her hands a little bit. "Can't have your hands falling off, now can we?" he asked with a solicitous grin. Turning to the kitchen and rummaging through a drawer he found a length of rope. This one seemed to be nylon. It was probably stronger than the coarse rope he had used earlier, but it was softer, too.

171

Albert walked behind her. He cut through the coarse rope, with some difficulty and let it fall to the floor around her feet. He also didn't tie her as tightly to the chair as he had the picnic table. If Kelly tried hard she might be able to get enough slack to work her way free, but it would take time. It would be easier with a knife. Where the thicker rope would have been pretty hopeless with anything but a super sharp blade, nylon would part easily with only a slightly sharp knife. She filed this away for later.

Kelly was tired and hurt all over from the last several hours of rough treatment. She was also famished, but wasn't under any illusion she would get something to eat soon. "Albert, could I please have some water?"

Albert looked up from where he was putting another log in the stove. He stood up slowly, like it pained him to do so. Limping over to the sink, he got her a glass of water and handed it to her without a word. He looked very tired. Kelly hoped he would take a nap so she could work on her bonds.

Kelly hadn't had many classes in psychology, but she thought that if she could get him talking he might let her go. She had been told by many a man that she was very persuasive. This wasn't the same kind of persuasion, but it was worth a try. Pretending concern, Kelly ventured, "So, how did you hurt your leg?"

"It got caught in a mine accident. It doesn't bother me unless I get tired," Albert replied shortly.

Kelly waited, but Albert didn't offer anything more so she ventured, "Oh, were you a miner?"

Albert gave her a strange look and sat down in a chair across from her. He thought a moment and seemed to come to a conclusion. "I guess I can tell you," he sighed, "you aren't going anywhere."

"My mom wasn't a very good mom," he continued. "She loved me, or so she said, but her job was more important than I was. She used to work long hours at a lawyer's office as a paralegal. I was left on my own for hours on end." Here Albert paused as if reliving those long, lonely evenings. "My dad was not in the picture after about the second year, so she had to raise me on her own. I still remember the long afternoons alone. I wasn't allowed to go over to a friend's house or have any of them over if mom wasn't home."

"That sounds like a lonely life," Kelly ventured in what she hoped sounded like a sympathetic voice.

Albert gave her another strange look. It was the kind of look that said she couldn't possibly understand, so why should she offer him sympathy? He was quiet for so long that Kelly was afraid he would stop speaking. Kelly shut her mouth and determined to keep it shut if he ever started speaking again.

"It wasn't just that she was never there, it was that when she was there it was hell," he paused and Kelly hoped he would elaborate, but instead Albert picked up the story where he left off, as if he had never been interrupted. "We lived in Arkansas. The hills are a treasure trove for a young boy. Unfortunately, they are also very dangerous. There are lots of caves, both explored and unexplored, and a few mines scattered about. I made forts in many of them and played in all of them in our area."

"One time my mother caught me. She used the belt on me, but it didn't stop me," Albert added with defiance and pride in his voice. "She warned me that if I got hurt, there would be no one to help her earn the extra money we needed to live."

Albert's voice got very monotone, with no emotion to it at all, and then he dropped a bombshell on my head, "You see mom turned tricks in the late evenings. At first it was okay, I just had to stay out of the way, but once I woke screaming, with a nightmare, and she beat me so badly that I couldn't go to school for two weeks, because of all the bruises. After that she was careful to never hit me in the face, and she never used the buckle of the belt again, only the leather end."

I was horrified, but Albert seemed not to notice my reaction and plowed with his story, "I was about 8 when one of her customers asked to have a go at me. She didn't even think of refusing, but I think she made more money if I was involved than she made just for her." Here he did pause and it was long moments before he went on, "but you have to understand, I was loved, fed and had plenty of clothes. And I did have my hills and caves to play in." No, Kelly, thought. She did not have to understand. A slow bubble of horror was surfacing in her for what that little boy had gone through.

"I just made extra sure she didn't discover my adventures after that. When I was eleven, I fell into a mine ventilation shaft. It had been left unsealed. When I hit the bottom my leg broke. I was trapped in that awful hole for 6 days and nights. Sometimes I heard searchers, but they couldn't hear me. I survived by drinking water that ran down the walls. But with nothing to eat I was very weak when they found me."

Albert had gotten more and more mechanical with his recitation. It was obvious he was remembering the moment as much as he was telling her the story. He had probably distanced himself from the emotional pain of it all. Kelly wasn't going to interrupt; she was captivated by his story. She couldn't imagine the pain and terror that little boy must have felt.

After a moment he continued, "When they finally found me, my mom wasn't even home. They had to call her at work to come see me. It took over three hours for her to get to the hospital. She explained or rather tried to explain her absence to me. How do you explain to your only son that you couldn't even be home for him because your job was more important? Or why you had to finish up at court before you came to see him after he almost died in a mine?"

"I didn't really listen to the excuses. I certainly didn't believe them." Albert paced, limping again. "She was not fit to be a mom. No woman is able to work in a professional job and also be a mom. I won't let that happen to some other kid!"

He stopped pacing, resting his leg. "My leg never healed quite right. It still pains me when I overuse it." He paused. "Growing up with a limp wasn't fun," he recalled. "Kids tease unmercifully in middle school, you know."

Kelly was bowled over by this story. Albert had probably started on his way to insanity well before the mine incident. The teasing and constant pain from his leg drove him the rest of the way over the edge. But it was a long way from that to murder. Kelly thought she might know why he was doing it, but she wanted to make sure her idea was right. She needed to know for sure what was driving him. It was the only way she might talk her way out of this mess.

Kelly broke the silence that had been hanging there for several minutes, "It is too bad your mom wasn't a good mother. I am sorry you had to go through that." Taking a small breath she lied a bit, "I don't think any woman should become a mother if she can't set aside her job for her family. I would never put my job ahead of my kid." Kelly thought fleetingly about the child she would never be able to have with Jack. She wanted him so bad. Jack, where are you?

"Oh, that is what you say now," Albert stated. He shook his finger at her, "but you lie!" He started pacing again. "You don't think you do, but you do. My mom told me she had intended to give up her career when I was born, but she hadn't. She tried to blame it on my dad, but I knew the truth. Mom loved her career, and those other men, more than me." He turned back toward her, angry, "All you career woman are the same," he snarled this last at her.

The madder he got, the more spittle came out of his mouth. With his next words she actually felt the moisture hit her in the face. "You all think you will put your kids first, but when it comes down to it, you won't. You have spent too much money on your careers, and you love them more than anything else in your life." He stopped his tirade here, and sat, but he was still fuming quietly to himself.

Kelly was afraid he was going to hit her, or worse, that he would kill her on the spot. She kept very still, eyes downcast so as not to challenge him at all. After a few moments, when no blows had landed, she ventured to look up again. Albert was holding a picture in his hands. She could see that it was worn and old, ragged on the edges. Kelly thought he must have pulled it out of his pocket, though she hadn't seen him do it.

He sat like that for a long time, looking at the picture, his fingers absently toying with the frayed edges. No emotions played across his face. Kelly couldn't begin to guess what he was feeling.

After a while Albert stretched and set the picture on the table. "I'll be back soon. You sit tight now," Albert said, with a laugh, as he got up. He put on his coat and strode to the door. Kelly hardly dared to breathe until the door clicked shut behind her. When she heard his car start she looked around for what she could use to escape.

Her eyes fell on the picture Albert had left. It was a picture of a middle aged woman. She looked rough around the edges, a few too many lines in her face, like life had not been kind to her. Her shoulders were back and her head held high, like she had been a proud woman. The auburn hair wasn't shiny, but it was shoulder length and left loose. She had kind blue eyes. Intuitively, Kelly had known she would see the resemblance to herself before she looked at the photo, but it was still sobering to see an older version of herself looking back at her. Absently, she wondered what had become of Albert's mother, knowing she didn't really want the answer.

Chapter Seventeen

Jack sat in his office, in front of the map. He pulled up internet sites about the Old Sign mine. Once a silver mine, it had long since stopped producing silver and had been fenced off and boarded up. Old ventilation shafts made the area unstable and unsafe. Jack shuddered as he imagined Kelly trapped by a cave-in.

The mine had several shafts and it would take too long to explore them all. Jack hoped he could find a trail to follow. Lady luck would have to help him out; he couldn't afford a further delay. He needed to bring his captain up to speed. Lights and rope would probably help too.

Jack picked up his phone and dialed the captain's office. On the fourth ring it went to voice mail. Jack hung up and dialed the captain's cell phone, before he remembered that the captain was out to a funeral for a distant family member. There was no time to find him to clear the operation; every second he delayed left Kelly in danger. Unless she was dead already.

Jack stopped that thought before it could fully form. He

replaced the mental image of her hanging from a tree with an image of him carrying her in his arms. Thrusting the negative images from his mind, he thought about making love to her. A vision of them on a wedding day. Their honeymoon, maybe in Hawaii or Mexico, someplace far from Albert. He just had to get to her. He would.

Jack grabbed up his map. Striding out of his office he headed for the supply lockers in the basement of the building. He jabbed the down button several times on the elevator before he gave up. Taking the stairs was faster. With his long strides eating up the steps two or three at a time, he was down the three floors in no time flat.

He quickly raided three lockers in the supply room—the first for rope, the second for a flashlight and the final one produced a sturdy hunting-type knife in a leather sheath. The rope he threw over his shoulder. The flashlight stayed in his hand, but the knife he strapped to his leg. Feeling as prepared as he could be, Jack headed for his car. The car contained a basic first aid kit, as well as flares and a blanket in case he was ever caught in a storm. Those would do for emergency supplies if he needed them.

Once in his car he pulled out of the garage and headed toward the canyon. Clouds covered the sky and a few snowflakes started to fall. It was going to be a serious storm, the first major snowstorm of the season to hit the lower country and it would have to pick today to come in. Great. Now he was fighting the weather as well as the clock. Hang on Kelly. Hang on my beloved.

Chapter Eighteen

Kelly snapped out of her contemplation of the picture. She didn't think she would have much time to herself. Albert had probably only left so she wouldn't see him upset, he'd be back soon. At least Kelly assumed that was why he'd left. She certainly hoped he wasn't going out to figure out where to dispose of her. Her great plan to get him talking had certainly backfired. Now he was even more agitated. Maybe it was good, because with his absence she had some time.

She peered out the window, verifying that he really was gone, not just sneaking back to see what she was doing. The sky was bright, but snow was falling. It looked to be a doozey of a storm. If she was going it would have to be soon; it would be a death sentence to try to wade through a blizzard up here.

Kelly's bonds made her legs fall asleep. Setting her teeth against the sharp pain, she placed her feet on the floor. The cold took her breath away. The stove had just taken the edge off the room, but Kelly was sure it was still about 50 degrees in there. It was painful to move at all. Her whole body felt like a stiff, unbending board, from sitting so long. The rocking motion that carried her to her feet caused a moan to slip out between tightly clinched lips. She rocked four times before finally coming to rest on her feet. It was a precarious position, bent over with a chair tied to her. Kelly felt like a kid trying to balance on the middle of a teeter-totter.

Shuffling forward, she barely managed to keep her feet the first couple of steps. It felt like she would fall at any moment. Kelly was sure that she would tip over on her side with no way to get back up. No way! She had to do this. She got herself into this mess and she would get herself out. Slowly, growing steadier as she went, she made her way to the kitchen and awkwardly started to open drawers.

The third drawer had what she needed, a sharp knife. Fortunately, the drawer was low enough that she could reach in with her bound hands, even with her chest tied to the chair. Kelly quickly grabbed the knife, shutting the drawer out of habit. Tipping precariously on her feet, she started when she heard a car crunching its tires over the gravel in the road. She almost panicked.

No! I was so close! It's not fair! Kelly thought. Angry, frustrated tears burned behind her tightly clinched eyes. Kelly kept it together the same way she had all day, sheer determination. She blinked back the tears and opened her eyes. Quickly she hobbled back to the fireplace and set her chair down where it had been before. Now her only problem was the knife in her hands. She looked around but couldn't find anywhere to stash it. She thought furiously.

The car door slammed shut and feet crunched on the new snow. Kelly slit her pants and slid the blade in. The door handle turned right as the knife handle slid out of sight. She hoped it was well enough hidden. She tried to calm her racing heart as the door opened and Albert limped inside with a bag of groceries in his arms. Kelly's tummy rumbled at the sight, loud enough for Albert to hear across the room. Where had he found a store so close?

"Yes, I will soon quiet your stomach," he said. "I hope you like steak and eggs for breakfast." Then looking at his watch on his arm he amended, with a little chuckle, "I mean lunch."

Kelly wanted to scream at him to let her go. She wanted to insist she wasn't like his mother. Instead she said, "That would be very nice, thank you." She really did not want to get him angry again. He seemed in a good mood, whatever the reason.

"Sorry I had to leave you so long. It won't happen again." Kelly's heart sank. Now she would have to wait until tonight to get loose. The snow continued to fall outside. They would probably have over a foot of fresh powder before morning. Albert continued, "I had to get to my mine and get this out of my refrigerator," Albert said. "No power up this high, I have to keep anything electric at the mine."

Kelly looked around and noticed for the first time that there was no refrigerator in the kitchen. She looked at the walls and noticed kerosene lamps instead of incandescent bulbs. Another fear nagged at the back of her brain, Albert lived so far off the grid that no one even knew this place was here. If by some miracle Jack did figure out where to look, he had no chance of finding her. Some small thought tickled her, nudging and insisting, but she couldn't chase it down right now.

Albert interrupted her internal search, "I'm a very good cook. My mom never had time to cook for me, so I learned how when I was very young and perfected it while I was healing from my broken leg." Kelly heard the sarcastic edge to his voice when he said the word, 'healing' and she was afraid he would lapse back into his earlier funk, but he didn't seem to. "Now, be quiet so I can get this going. It takes some time to cook on this stove."

Kelly didn't mind giving him quiet or having his attention directed somewhere else. Albert was not only insane, but his strange bi-polar moods gave her the creeps. Since his mood swings could get her killed, she really wanted to keep him calm. Instead of focusing on it she decided to try to figure out what was bothering her.

Kelly relaxed as much as the ropes would let her. She took three deep breaths, then another and finally one more. Closing her eyes she allowed herself to go into a bit of a trance; a very relaxed state. She followed the feeling until it started to become more solid. The first image that came to mind was wonderful so she went with it. Jack holding her gently in his arms. The two of them joined as only lovers could. Rocking back and forth together in the age old song and dance of love. This wonderful feeling was replaced by an anxiety. She had to tell him about her failing, but this time when she relived it the outcome was different. In her head she was saying the words, "It was all my fault," but in her heart she knew it wasn't true.

That was what had been tickling her mind, demanding attention. The realization almost snapped her out of her self-induced trance. Paul had not planned it out very well. If he really suspected the person at the door to be dangerous he should never have opened it. They shouldn't have had the gun so far away. The situation was not ideal. She was untrained, but even trained, she couldn't have stopped the murder. She might have been able to kill the bastard that killed Paul, but even that would have been dangerous and would have been too late to help Paul. It was not her fault Paul had died.

When Kelly had been kidnapped, it wasn't Jack's fault. He couldn't have stopped it from happening, even if he had been her back up. He probably couldn't have rescued her either. If she died it wouldn't be his fault. There was just no way he could get to her in time to help. Kelly's eyes finally flew open; she came completely out of her trance. Had Albert been looking, he would have wondered what the small smile was on her face. Albert would have been curious about why she looked relieved and less tense. Kelly was even more determined to escape and tell Jack that she had been wrong. It wasn't her fault Paul died. She couldn't have stopped the murder, then or even with the extra training she had now.

Jack had been so mad at her. Now Kelly could see that anger for what it had been. Surely Jack had been upset that she was blaming herself. At best he would have seen it as an attention-getting stunt and pushed her away. At worst he would have seen her as a person who needed therapeutic help. He would have felt he couldn't afford to get involved with her. When she escaped and was in his arms again she would prove to him she was worth loving. Worth the risk. It was worth any effort from her to just feel his strong arms around her again. She wanted to collapse into his chest and just listen to his heart beat. She loved him, had always loved him, would always love him, and now just needed to get away so she could make sure he knew it.

Jack stopped at the local camping outfitters on the way out of town to pick up two days of dehydrated food. With all the moisture from the snowstorm he wouldn't need water, just extra matches and fuel to start a fire. Paying for them with his department credit card, he asked for an extra plastic bag and ran to the car. The extra bag would also keep the matches dry if he had to hike in the storm that was moving in.

Jack had to slow to a crawl up the canyon and he cursed the weather soundly. The canyon roads were icy and slick. Several cars pulled over to put on chains. Jack had chains, too, but didn't want to waste the time putting them on. Traffic was crawling, but Jack kept a good distance from the car in front of him. He eased his car over the slight rise and onto the downhill after mile marker five. The car in front of him started into an uncontrolled slide. Pumping his breaks, trying to create more distance between himself and the other driver, Jack's car didn't respond. He pumped them faster. The car took notice of the request to slow, but decided to turn sideways in the road instead.

By now the car in front of him was sideways and blocking half the canyon. Jack slid, miraculously, around the stopped car in front of him. Cranking the wheel madly in the direction of the skid Jack finally convinced his BMW to turn the other way, but he overshot straight. Where he had been traveling at a crawl of 5 mph when he topped the hill he noticed he was now doing 15 mph and picking up speed. The guard rail stood between Jack and the river. Thank goodness for the guard rail, Jack thought, as the nose of his car brushed up against it. After what seemed like hours, the slow motion accident was over. Jack got out of his car and looked up the hill he had just come down. There were four cars in various states of disarray on the road. His seemed to be the only one that had actually hit something. Everyone seemed to be okay.

From his trunk Jack grudgingly removed the chains and proceeded to get thoroughly wet and miserable putting the things on his two back tires. Jack couldn't waste any more time worrying about the other cars. They were all safe, even if the traffic jam would take hours to clear. Jack had to get to Kelly.

Albert's voice woke Kelly, who had been snoozing a little, despite the discomfort of her situation. "I hope you like your steak medium. I got tired of trying to get it to cook more." Carrying two heaping plates to the chair across from her he sat down. He set one in her lap and Kelly cringed, afraid he would find the knife she had hidden. She needn't have worried though; it seemed Albert wasn't going to touch her. It was like she had the plague or something.

Kelly waggled her bound hands at Albert, they couldn't reach her mouth. Hopefully he would untie her. She thought rapidly, planning how to use her hidden knife to fight her way free when the time came. These hopes were quickly dashed when Albert picked up the fork and started shoveling the already cut pieces of meat into her mouth. He alternated, feeding her and taking a bite of his own to give her time to chew.

He did not give her time to talk. Albert said nothing at all during their meal and the couple of times Kelly tried he shoved food in her mouth too quickly for her to get more than one word out. Kelly finally took the hint and stayed quiet.

Albert picked up the dishes and headed to the kitchen sink with them. Quietly, he scraped off the plates and washed them. Outside the window, Kelly could see that the sun was already past its zenith, and the snow was starting to pile up. She was pretty sure that it was already six inches deep and headed for a foot or more. Her situation was perilous and getting worse by the minute. But her head was foggy and she couldn't keep her eyes open. Exhausted by the long night, with a full belly lulling her, Kelly fell asleep where she sat.

There was no road to the mine from the highway. Jack would have to park on the side of the road. Jack slowed his car, trying to judge the depth of the snow in the turnout where he thought he needed to park. It looked deep, but soft. Hopefully he would be able to get his car back out. Jack carefully edged his car into the pullout, really not much more than a wider spot on the shoulder of the canyon road.

Jack made sure his headlights were off. He might need to leave in a hurry, and a dead battery wouldn't do. Gathering his supplies, he dumped Kelly's supplies out of her backpack and tossed in the bag from the camping store. The rope, flashlight and knife went on top where he could get at them. With any luck he wouldn't need any of it, but it was best to be prepared.

Jack looked up the steep slope of land containing the Old Signe Mine. He knew the mine ran through these hills for a long way, not miles, but more than he would want to try to explore in one day. Jack set off up the steep hill. The mine entrance was supposed to be about 200 yards up the hill. Presumably there was a path leading to the entrance, but with the snow and the fact no one ever came here anymore, he couldn't find the trail.

For every few steps he took up the hill he slid back some. The ground was slick under the snow. Fall snows were often like that. Jack cursed his luck for not remembering to bring his crampons. He was wasting time; time he didn't have to waste.

Finally, Jack reached a chain link fence. It seemed to go on for as far as he could see, which admittedly wasn't far because of the trees and snow. He clung to the fence as he followed it up the hill. Pulling with his arms as much as pushing with his legs made for slow progress, but it was much better than without the handholds. The lack of a trail bothered him. If Kelly had been brought this way, the snow had covered their tracks.

The steep hill was tiring and Jack finally had to stop for a minute. He took great big gulping breaths. His feet were ice cold and his tennis shoes felt wet. How could he have been so unprepared? It wasn't like he was new to hiking in the winter in Boulder County. Obviously he had been in just too much of a hurry. Nothing to do now but see it through. The highway might close at any time, making it impossible for him to get home for better gear. Or if he did get home, he might not be able to make it back to the mine. Jack looked at his watch, saying some choice words when he saw it was after three. He only had about three hours before dark. Not much time to pull off the rescue. Once it got dark the roads would be impassable with the ice build-up. He would be hours getting Kelly to the help she might need.

With time pushing him even harder, he forced himself on. A moment later he saw a gap in the fence. It looked like a gate had been there at one time, but the posts the gate would have been connected to were rusted and twisted, like someone had hit them with a sledge hammer until the gate gave way. There were tons of people who squatted on the vacant land in this area. It wasn't surprising someone had broken down the gate. Maybe even Albert, whoever he was.

Once through the fence, it was easy to see the gated entrance to the mine. Jack felt hopeless, not at all sure he could get through a lock. As he moved closer, he saw that the lock was missing. Someone, probably the same person, had busted the lock off. All Jack had to do was pull on it and he thought it would open.

Jack glanced furtively over his shoulder. He didn't see anyone, or even any foot prints, but they would have disappeared pretty quickly in the snow. Jack slowly pulled on the gate. Surprisingly, it swung open noiselessly on well-oiled hinges. Jack drew his gun and stepped inside.

The mine entrance opened up almost immediately to a large chamber. Moving to one side, Jack crept carefully forward, keeping the wall against his left shoulder. There was plenty of light seeping into the room from the entrance. Jack paused, looking around and listening intently. It was amazing the amount of junk in the room. There were tools of all descriptions, some of which he recognized, like a circular saw and jigsaw. Most he didn't recognize, probably related to mining. They were mostly rusted hulks left to decay on their tracks or wheels.

Jack was intrigued by the refrigerator sitting against one wall. It was humming quietly, like the compressor was running. Jack walked up to it. He looked it over for a minute, puzzled as to why it was there. Opening the door he found a half eaten sandwich inside. A quick inventory also showed milk, vegetables and meat. None of it was spoiled, so whoever was using it had done so recently. Jack quickly shut the door and got on to his exploration of the mine.

Moving along the same wall, Jack paused at what appeared to be the main shaft leading deeper into the mine. It was a guess, but Jack felt pretty sure he should take the most travel-worn path. This main branch was the largest and gave every indication it was used the most, a groove worn in the dirt between the old rusty rails. Jack felt his heart race as he contemplated the dark opening in front of him. Electric lights were strung on the walls, but they were turned off.

He reached up to feel one. It was slightly warm, like it had been on not too long ago. Jack wished he knew how long ago that 'not too long ago' was. Taking his flashlight out of the pack, he switched it on. Holding the flashlight in his left hand, he kept his gun in his right. He regretted deviating from his training, but he needed both hands for balance on the rough ground. They had drilled it into him to hold the flashlight pointed the same way as the gun. He was supposed to do this by holding the gun in his right hand on top of the flashlight in his left. This was because when an officer saw a bad guy he tended to pull the trigger. So if he saw the bad guy with the light and his gun was pointed elsewhere he might shoot something, or worse, someone, he didn't mean to by reflex.

Carefully making his way down the tunnel, Jack kept glancing behind him, as well as keeping a sharp lookout to the front. It was difficult to divide his focus. A feeling that he had to hurry made him even crazier. Jack felt the snow falling outside like a physical pressure pressing him to go faster. Between the snow and the killer's M.O., Jack was sure Kelly was running out of time.

Jack switched his flashlight off as an experiment. It was very dark now. The tunnel had taken so many twists and turns the natural light had faded completely. He felt comfortable he could find his way out again simply by following the most used passages. Jack yearned to call out to Kelly, but didn't dare. No matter how dark it was, Jack wasn't sure that Albert was gone. He might be standing over Kelly right now. If Albert suspected Jack was coming what would he do to Kelly? Jack didn't want to think about it.

Jack glanced at his watch. He had been moving slowly, carefully. When he saw that it was already 4:30 he realized he had been moving too slowly, too carefully. He would have to take a chance and move faster. Hurrying up his steps to try to cover more distance, his instincts told him he was getting closer. Albert wouldn't have wanted to drag someone too far into the mine. It would be too much work. Most searchers would have given up by now. Many wouldn't have even seen the refrigerator hiding in among the other junk in the main room.

With his thoughts drifting, Jack was surprised as his foot snagged on something and he tripped. His flashlight and gun went flying down the tunnel just as the world exploded around him. A large boulder came zipping by him; right where his head had been moments before. His light hit the ground and went out. Curling into a ball, he put his hands behind his neck, protecting his head with his arms. When the rumble settled down he slowly uncurled. His ears were ringing from the explosion, but he was afraid to try to say anything for fear he might alert Albert. At least Jack was pretty sure it was Albert who set the blast.

In the flash of the explosion, Jack thought he saw an empty cot and maybe a chair behind the rock fall. He was pretty sure he had stumbled over a trip wire. There was not a single good reason Jack could think of that Albert might have set up a trap that would lock Albert and Kelly underground for good. Jack had to believe that Kelly wasn't here after all. Maybe this was just a hiding place for Albert. A place he went just to hang out, or feel safe, or do whatever insane serial murderers needed a place like this for.

Jack felt like an idiot. An idiot without a gun. He had been so sure that Kelly would be held in this mine. What a waste of valuable time. Not only did he have no idea where Albert was, but no new clues had turned up either. He needed Kelly, couldn't survive without her. She was his only love, his soul mate.

Jack could feel the weight of the rock pushing down on him. He wasn't buried, but it felt like it. Using monumental effort he stood up carefully.

After testing his weight on both feet he reached out to find the wall he had been near. As his hand brushed the wall, Jack was able to get his breathing under control and take stock of his surroundings by feel.

The way he had been going was totally blocked by rock. He still had Kelly's pack with his supplies, and he wasn't physically damaged. However, he didn't have his light. He had no idea where Kelly was. He had no idea how much time they had left. Jack was as close to complete despair as he had ever been in his life.

Chapter Nineteen

A quiet distant rumble woke Kelly from a fitful snooze. Albert was already headed for his coat by the time Kelly blinked the sleep out of her eyes and remembered where she was. "What was that?" she asked.

"Someone snooped too far into my private sanctum. They tripped the wire and sprung the trap I had set. I guess someone was getting too close to finding you." Hope flared in her chest, but Kelly's hope was short lived. Albert shattered it when he finished, "I wonder if they had any idea what hit them before they died?"

Albert never heard her sobs because he was already out the door. Kelly didn't waste long crying over Jack; she needed to get out of there before Albert came back. He would only be gone for a few minutes if last time was anything to judge by.

Straining her fingers to reach into the small slit in her pants, just above the knee, Kelly carefully slipped the knife out of its precarious hiding place. She reflected that she was lucky it hadn't been found by Albert when he fed her. When she woke from her nap it had been the first thing she felt for. She was fortunate that she didn't cut herself with the sharp blade as the knife was pulled out flat along her leg.

Gripping the knife between her knees she worked her wrists up and down, dragging the rope along the blade. Stopping every few strokes to reposition the knife so it wouldn't fall was frustrating. The nylon rope was more stubborn than she expected, but it finally separated. Kelly spared a moment to rub her wrists to help get the blood flowing again. When her fingers started to tingle she switched her efforts to the rope around her chest. Her wrists screamed from bending but Kelly managed to work the knife between her sternum and the rope with the blade side out. She carefully sawed up and down, her hands and arms protesting the effort. When the rope finally parted Kelly tumbled to the floor.

The tears came back full force. She was free, but she hurt all over from holding still so long. Kelly marshaled her thoughts, damping the emotions, and concentrated on escaping. She entertained a few fleeting thoughts of revenge, but knew she would never follow through with them. The only man she cared about was dead. Or was he? Could she believe Albert? Maybe it wasn't Jack. Maybe a bear had set off the trap. If that were so it was all the more important for Kelly to escape. It meant that there was a chance Jack was still out there.

Kelly clawed her way to her feet, using the chair for support. She pushed off the chair and stood on her own. By moving carefully, one painful step at a time, she was able to walk. It would be a few minutes before she would be able to run. Kelly felt the urgency to escape like a physical thing pushing at her to move. Nevertheless she took the time to search for some shoes.

There were none to be found. She did find a lightweight wind breaker in one corner, and slipped it on over her head. On her way across the room to search the kitchen for anything she could use, like matches, she saw the blanket on the bed. She grabbed it, found matches and a pair of scissors from the kitchen and ran out the door. She would need to fashion wraps for her feet, but she wanted to be long gone from the cabin before she slowed down. Kelly stumbled out into the crisp air. It wasn't super cold yet, but Kelly knew it would be soon.

Jack continued to walk carefully out of the mine, slowly feeling his way along the walls. He wanted to run. He wanted to atone for his mistakes, to take Kelly into his arms, and tell her he loved her. He wanted to start this whole week over again and do things differently. Instead he had to be content with slowly making his way out of the mine. It chafed him to be so impotent.

Was that a noise? Jack paused to listen. He was sure of it now. A shuffling step echoed through the tunnel. It sounded like some kind of animal was coming at him. No, it was too purposeful. Maybe a person walking? Jack wasn't sure, but he knew he needed to hide. Just as a beam of light came around the corner Jack found a side corridor and hunkered down in it. The beam flickered past his hiding place and a person limped by. The man was not too tall, and seemed determined to get where he was going. Probably headed to the trap. When the man's flashlight lit up the side tunnel, Jack got a good chance to look around his surroundings. It was a good thing he did, too.

Behind Jack, by about two feet, was a dark hole in the floor. After Albert went by, Jack scurried to the hole and, lying on his tummy, he stuck an arm in as far as it would reach. Not only did he not feel a bottom, but he also felt cool air wafting up at him. Jack guessed it was a ventilation shaft to deeper levels in the mine. Jack seemed to recall that these shafts could be hundreds of feet deep. Had he gone further back from the main tunnel, he'd be dead. The thought was chilling. He couldn't continue to try to make his way out without a light; he'd have to wait for Albert's. He was also pretty sure he had seen a gun in Albert's hand when he walked by.

"Come on Jack," he whispered under his breath. He had to figure out what to do. He had an idea, a brilliant, but dangerous idea. It would involve him going deeper into the side tunnel; with no light to see by, he ran the risk of falling into a similar shaft. To make it more complicated, the floor was littered with large rocks; the footing unstable. It would also mean getting past the shaft without falling in.

Kelly's feet burned from the cold bite of the snow as she made her way away from the cabin. She looked for a good place to jump off the road. She wanted somewhere to hide, but didn't want to leave tracks for Albert to find. As long as she stayed in the tire tracks her trail was hidden.

About 50 steps down the road she saw a tree encroaching on the road with a large boulder beside it. She carefully wrapped her blanket tight about herself and jumped as far as she could. Landing behind the boulder, her frozen feet and battered body refused to support her, tumbling her into the snow. She lay there panting for a moment, until the seeping wetness got her moving. The melting snow was cold! Her feet burned. She brushed some snow off of a smallish rock and sat on the blanket. Her feet were bright red, but quickly loosing feeling now. Kelly knew it was not a good sign, but she was grateful for relief of the pain.

Using the scissors, Kelly cut strips from the blanket. She used those strips to bind her feet. As she worked, Kelly kept a close eye out for the returning car. Every second that she didn't see it or hear its rumbling made her more tense. She was sure she was running out of time. Albert would be back. She had to get further from the road. She had to get further away, where Albert wouldn't see her when he came back. It would be dark soon and that would hide her movements. The snow falling from the sky would cover her steps, but not for a little while yet. Kelly walked away from the road.

Jack started by shifting his weight carefully over the hole in front of him. He eased his hands to the other side and crab-walked his feet over. On the other side, he paused, satisfied. The hole stood between him and a crazy guy carrying a gun. Jack carefully crawled further into the side tunnel. He had seen a bend he hoped he could hide behind. Jack was relieved that he had been right.

Jack found a good size rock, by feel alone. He gripped it in his right hand and balanced himself with his left. He sat perfectly still and waited. It wasn't a long wait. Albert came back along the corridor whistling quietly, obviously very happy with himself. He must have surmised that the cave-in had buried Jack. Jack smiled a tight smile of his own, thinking about how wrong Albert was.

Jack let out a loud moan and called out, "Help me!" in a voice that carried, but sounded weak and desperate at the same time. "Someone out there? Anyone? Please help me?" He moaned again for good measure.

It worked. The whistling stopped and the shuffling step stopped. Jack moaned again; waited. He was pretty sure Albert would take the bait, but if he didn't Jack would have to escape the side corridor and try to take on Albert and his gun in the main corridor. Kelly couldn't wait. Jack couldn't let Albert get away. Jack rocked his weight forward onto the balls of his feet. His calves coiled to spring around the corner and get out into the main passage before all light fled.

Jack was so ready to spring that when he heard a voice call out, "I'll help you, just stay where you are," he almost shot out of the side tunnel. It would have been a fatal mistake. Jack could see the light shining against the wall where his tunnel turned. He moaned again for good effect calling out, "I think my leg is broken, help me please!"

The light became less intense as Albert shifted the beam more to his feet and less down the corridor. Jack risked a glance around the corner. Albert was making his way slowly into the side tunnel. For good measure Jack let out a scream of agony. Albert looked up, saw Jack. Jack saw Albert's gun come up; saw Albert take an unsteady step toward him. It was like a slow motion film. Albert's dragging leg caught on a loose stone about the size of a loaf of bread. It was enough to trip Albert. Albert's flashlight went tumbling through the air as he reached out to catch himself on the non-existent floor. Jack saw the macabre sight in flashes as the light tumbled in circles. Albert's gun went off with a roar.

Deafened again by the gun shot, Jack couldn't even hear the man's scream as he tumbled into the shaft. Jack flinched at the sight. Knowing it had almost been him that fell into the shaft, he took an involuntary step forward. Suddenly, it went dark. The flashlight had gone out when it hit the ground. He cursed his luck. Now he had to make his way back across the shaft and out of the tunnel with no light, right back where he started.

Jack grabbed his emergency supply pack and started forward on hands and knees again. He had no interest in joining Albert in the shaft. The middle finger of his right hand hit something hard, but smooth. A flare of light pierced the darkness as Albert's flashlight flared to life. The light was both a boon and a curse. Now he could see where to place his hands and feet as he crawled over the pit, but his heart also skipped a beat as the light beam faded into its depths.

The first thing Jack did when he was back in the main tunnel was check his watch. It was 5:30. Jack knew it would be dark outside now and he had no idea where to look for Kelly.

Kelly stumbled a bit. She knew if she kept moving she had a chance. Her body screamed at her to rest. Her will urged her on. She had to survive. She had to hope that it had not been Jack in that mine, believing with all her heart that he was waiting for her, that she could tell him how she felt. How much of a fool she had been. How she wanted to spend the rest of her life with him, even if it meant not being a detective anymore.

Kelly could no longer feel her feet at all. She stumbled on dead stumps instead of legs. She could still see the road off to her right about 100 feet away. It beckoned to her. An easier path to follow, lighter snow, due to the packed down tire treads. She longed to walk over there, in comparable comfort. The heavy snow drifts were making it hard to go on. She stumbled again banging her toe on some rock or root. She couldn't tell which toe, she only knew her foot stopped moving and plunged her into the snow again. Her blanket was totally covered in snow. She looked like an abominable snowman patrolling the woods.

Kelly's feet headed for the road, her brain temporarily forgetting the danger there. Why couldn't she walk in the road? The road would lead to safety. 'No!' part of her mind screamed, it would lead to death. She turned back away, not remembering why, but she couldn't go near the road. Her world was narrowing rapidly. Her thoughts focused on putting one foot in front of the other. She couldn't even remember why she was out walking in the snow, except to get away. It was very important she get away.

Kelly trudged on for several more minutes. Her world tapering to whiteness. Her steps drifting again toward the road, toward safety. No, danger! Her mind wasn't clear, she couldn't focus it at all. Why would the road be dangerous? She was only about 50 feet from it now. Surely it would be easier to travel on the road. The white path begged her to come to it.

Jack made quick work of escaping the mine now that he had a flashlight. His fast walk turned into a run when he left the mine entrance. There was a car parked just outside the fence. It had only a dusting of snow; it must be Albert's. The sky was darkening fast. Jack glanced at his watch. It read 5:55. Only half an hour until it would be really dark. If he hurried, he could follow the tracks the car had left. Veering toward the tracks, Jack reasoned that they would lead to Kelly. By the time he found her it would be dark, they would be on foot, and she could be injured. Already, it was getting difficult to tell the road from the surrounding country.

Jack made a quick decision and turned his run toward the car itself. Slipping, he slid into the side of the car. The slight pain was ignored as he had a horrible thought. What if Albert had the keys with him when he fell down the ventilation shaft? Jack would have to back track to his car and hope to find the road from the highway. Opening the car door Jack discovered that Albert had left the keys in it and it was a Subaru Legacy, all-wheel drive. Thank goodness!

Jack held his breath as he started the car. He needn't have worried; it started right up. From the sound it needed a new muffler, but nothing else seemed amiss. Jack took off care-fully in the direction the car had come from. He hoped he found Kelly quickly.

Jack saw nothing but whiteness for about a mile, which took him a frustrating five minutes to drive. Even with his reduced speed he knew he would hit anything standing in the road. The tires on the car just weren't good enough to give him great stopping power. Nevertheless Jack slammed on the brakes when he saw a dark shape in the road ahead of him.

Kelly had not made it to the road, yet, when she heard a distant noise; she froze in place, like a rabbit caught in the headlights of a car. She recognized the sound of a car. For some reason the car terrified her. She dove for cover, hiding under the blanket behind a fallen tree. The sound of the car, or the fall, jarred away some of the cobwebs. Kelly remembered. She remembered it all and was very afraid. She hid until the car drove out of sight the way she had come, then she stood up and ran. Kelly was out of time and she knew it.

Jack was amazed to find the cabin, out here in the middle of nowhere. The road seemed to end at it, but maybe it actually went around and he couldn't see it for all the snow. The car drifted to a full stop just scant feet from the front door. He jumped out of the car. Running to the front door, he jerked it open and took in the scene before him with sinking heart. It was deserted.

First he noticed the kitchen. No refrigerator. That must be why Albert kept one at the mine. Out of his peripheral vision he noted a comfortable looking chair near the fire. Turning, he saw the other chair. Across from the first there was a folding chair that had ropes laying at its feet, both coarse and nylon.

Jack ran forward, and picked up a light brown, thick, rough rope fragment. It was the same rope used in all three of the murder scenes. His heart beat faster. Next he picked up the nylon strand. Examining the end of this rope he noticed it was frayed, like it a mouse had gnawed through it. Obviously it had taken someone a long time to cut through it. He had some hope, that Kelly had cut her way free instead of being hauled off to a worse fate.

Kelly didn't make it far. She could feel that she was running slowly. Her body just wouldn't respond to her commands. She was out of adrenaline to help with the flight response she felt. As she willed her feet to take another step she knew they wouldn't. She tumbled head first into the snow, knowing that Albert would find her. Even if he didn't, the snow would claim her. Even knowing this, she still couldn't work up the energy to move. It was so warm in the snow. It would feel so good to take a little nap. She could use the rest. Only for a moment. She would close her eyes, only for a moment, then she would get up and keep running. Yes, that sounded fine. Kelly's eyes closed. She wasn't even aware of the car returning.

Jack searched around outside the house. He couldn't find any footprints or other sign of Kelly. He hadn't seen her on the drive from the mine to the house, but he had no hope of finding her if she had struck off cross country. Panic started to creep up his chest, threatening to choke him. If complete darkness fell, he would never find her. She hadn't been wearing a warm coat when she went to the school, and he was pretty sure she wouldn't be wearing one now. He stood rooted to the spot, his mind spinning.

He made up his mind. He would take the car, but drive slowly, with the windows down and look for her off the road. On the way to the mine, he'd search the left side, and come back searching the right side. He would also call for her. Maybe she was afraid and hiding.

Having a plan centered Jack. He headed for the car. Driving down the road at a crawl he searched as far as he could see off the road. Half a mile from the cabin something caught his eye off the road; a darker lump that looked like any other small boulder, except only half of it was covered in snow. Jack yelled, "Kelly! Kelly! Where are you?" There was no response.

Running from the car to the boulder was difficult. The snow was really getting deep. The closer Jack got to the lump, the more certain he was that it was a body; he could see a blanket now. He slid the last few steps on his knees, fearing the worst. Jack knelt beside the blanket-covered body and braced himself.

He gently removed the blanket, shaking the snow off it. As he feared, and hoped, it was Kelly. She was white as a sheet. At first he thought she wasn't breathing, but then he noticed the slight rise and fall of her chest. A sob escaped his lips when he noticed her bare feet. Lifting her into his arms he murmured into her ear, "Kelly, my love, I am so sorry. Don't leave me Kelly. I can't live without you."

Jack kept up his sweet murmurs as he carried her back to the car. Gently, he placed her into the passenger seat, but she slumped over into the drivers' seat. Jack shut the door, being careful of her feet, and hurried to slide into his seat. He lifted her head into his lap as gently as he could. Cranking the windows shut and turning the heat up to high, he set off for the cabin. There was no hope of finding a way out of these mountains with this much snow falling. It might be days before he could get Kelly to a hospital.

Kelly was dreaming. It was such a nice dream. Jack was there. He was telling her that he loved her. He rescued her. His strong arms carrying her to safety and to warmth. He laid her on a bed. Somewhere in all this she was vaguely aware that it wasn't a dream. Kelly was actually safe. She was with Jack and he loved her. "I love you, too," she whispered to him. She wasn't sure he heard. She tried again, but he was already gone. She drifted back to sleep, knowing she was safe.

Jack slammed the door of the cabin open with his foot. He set Kelly on the bed. The only thing he had to cover her with was the blanket from the car, which he made record time getting. Kelly moaned as he wrapped her in it. She didn't seem conscious, so he left her there and went to stoke the fire. He wanted it roaring to help bring up her core temperature. Coaxing the flames high enough to turn the little cabin into a sweat lodge, he returned to Kelly. He uncovered her. Her clothes were still mostly ice, not water. He set about stripping her out of them.

Kelly woke dimly aware of her surroundings. Jack was with her. He was stripping her. She tried to protest that now was not the time. Her feeble attempts to push him off failed miserably. She really didn't want him to stop, but she was way too tired to make out. She was so cold.

"Kelly, it's me Jack. You're going to be okay. I'm here. I'll never let you go again. I promise. I'll take care of you."

"Please, just be quiet and hold me," Kelly protested Jack's murmurs. She just wanted to sleep.

Jack stripped and crawled into the bed with her. Her ice cold body pressed against his warm one. It was like holding an ice cube. He pulled the cover up over them and held her tightly. She snuggled against him and fell asleep. Jack didn't think he could sleep, but as Kelly's body started to warm and the cabin got hotter he fell into a deep sleep.

Shortly after midnight Jack got out of bed to stoke the fire. Kelly was still asleep, but she looked better. Her skin was pink and she looked like she was resting comfortably. Jack carefully, so as not to wake her, looked at her toes and feet with a flashlight. Amazingly there was no black discoloration. She wouldn't lose any flesh to frost bite. Jack was astonished at her fortitude. He snuck back into the small bed to hold her once again. He drifted to sleep thinking how wonderful she felt in his arms.

Chapter Twenty

Kelly stirred and mumbled into Jack's shoulder. His body was warm, a bit of heaven after a long day in hell. She snuggled deeper into his embrace. Rolling onto her side and wrapping one leg over his waist she felt him responding to the pressure of her leg. She rested there a moment, enjoying the feel of him. Naked skin against naked skin. It was indeed bliss.

Jack was roused, in more ways than one, by Kelly's leg against his body. He could feel himself getting hard. As she moaned into his shoulder and rubbed her hands on his chest he responded more. Soon he wouldn't be able to go back to sleep even if he wanted to. Jack reached for her and pulled her on top of him.

Kelly rocked back and forth, up and down on his hardening member. She was getting very wet and he was promising to use that to its fullest. Last time had been too fast. This time she would make him beg by drawing it out as long as she could stand it, but that meant slowing down the rhythmic beat of her libido.

Her hips slowed their movement and she rolled a bit off of him. She wanted to navigate every inch of him with her hands. It was totally dark in their bedroom. But that was okay because Kelly enjoyed working by feel. Her fingers traced a gentle pattern on his lips; traveled down his throat to his chest. Kelly lingered there, drawing lazy figure eights with her finger nail. Gently, ever so gently she ran her nail around the nipples on his chest.

When her fingers had done their work on his hard pecs, Kelly continued on down his stomach, rolling her fingers over his six pack abs, to the strong straight dick nestled just below his fur. She ran her finger up one side and down the other laughing a little as he moaned with the pleasure of it. He stood even more at attention than he had. Kelly gave in a little and allowed her mouth to trail after her hands. Her tongue sought the soft places in his hard lines. Finally her lips came to rest around his erect head. She sucked a bit, but didn't want to get too rhythmic yet.

Jack was going crazy at her touch. He wanted her so badly that his shaft was standing straight up like the mast on a ship. A moan escaped when she pulled her mouth off. He couldn't let her continue to tease him. It was time for him to give some back.

He pushed her off of him, completely, rolling her onto her back. It was his turn to sit up on one elbow and tease her. Her skin felt soft under his touch. He stroked it gently, urging her skin to rise up to meet his fingers. Goosebumps sprung up under his fingers. He let his hands wander over her breasts and down her tight stomach. Caressing, encouraging, wanting to touch more of her, his hand slid gently between her legs.

Kelly was going to explode. He was teasing her with his fingers. She didn't know her body would enjoy being touched like this. Goosebumps rouse on her skin; her flesh asking for more contact. She shivered deliciously. His body warm against her side radiated love and warmth. When his fingers skittered down her body she thought she would lose control totally. She moaned as his fingers sought out the warm spot between her legs. Her sex screamed for his attention; fluids moistened her thighs.

She couldn't stand it and reached to pull him on top of her. Her hands slipped over smooth muscle. "Not, yet," he whispered in a husky voice. His voice said he wanted her. She needed him. She needed to hear his breath in her ear. Needed to feel the weight of his body on hers.

Jack gently dodged her grasping hands. He slipped down toward her feet in one smooth motion. Dragging his hands down the length of her body he knelt on the floor as his hands reached her feet. Working his fingers over the rough flesh, now warm from the comfort of both their bodies in bed, he rubbed gently. He heard a faint moan from her.

Kelly was sure she was being tortured in the best way possible. His gentle, insistent touch on her feet was almost as erotic as the earlier exploration of her body had been. As his hands traveled up her legs she melted into the bed. His fingers kneading her calf muscles and gently insisting she spread her thighs apart sent her to new levels of anticipation. She felt the bed shift as he climbed back up putting a slight weight on her legs. She reached for him again, intending to pull him up and into her. Her body seeking release.

Jack knew she wanted him. He throbbed with need for her, too. Strengthening his resolve to do this right and to take it slow he slowly inched his way up her thighs. His mouth watered at the thought that soon her juices would be running down his chin and coating his mouth. He needed to take her sex into his mouth. He needed to consume her. He didn't register the hands pulling at him. He was too intent on his goal.

Kelly grasped and tried to get a grip on his back to pull him up. Her hands ineffectual against his hard body. Now she could feel his erection again, hard against her feet. She teased him with her toes and rubbed his warm hard member with her foot. She needed him. A moan escaped her lips as she realized what he was going to do. The warmth from his tongue flicking over her clit was like a roaring fire. It stirred her to new heights of passion. He paused, looking up at her from between her legs.

He loved the taste of her. He had to have more of her, devour her. Just before plunging his tongue into her, he pulled back and looked her right in the eyes. He was happy to see she was watching him, with a pleased and surprised look on her face. He whispered, "I love you," just loud enough for her to hear. He plunged his mouth back onto her mound, sucking and investigating with his tongue.

The exquisite slowness of his explorations was going to push her over the edge. Had he actually just said that he loved her? He wanted him to say it so badly that she almost thought it was part of a delusion. But his tongue and the marvelous things it was doing to her was no delusion. Her body ached under his mouth. Her womanhood questing for more. She felt the orgasm rising within her. Her hands jerked on his back, seeking a grip. Fingers skittering over his flesh, she slipped to the bed; she clung tightly to the sheets. When her body released the bottled up energy, bolts of lightning shooting up her spine, she opened her mouth and screamed, "Jack! Oh, Jack, yes, yes, YES!"

Jack loved hearing her scream his name. His shaft jumped hard against her leg as he released her from his slow torture. Before her sex could stop quivering he gave a quick flick of his tongue over her swollen clit. His body was demanding release to match hers. He could no longer resist as her hands found him again and pulled him up. He let his body rub up the length of her stomach and chest, until he could slide gently into her.

Kelly was still reeling from the most intense orgasm of her life when he flicked her again with his tongue. The intensity of the spasm the worked its way up her body from her toes to her head was almost too much to take. His smooth skin was rubbing over her legs as he scooted up her body. Her hands shifted to his arms, encouraging him upward. His arms were flexed and hard from taking the weight of his body off of her.

She wanted his cum in her. She had to feel him like he had felt her. She had to know he loved her. She wanted to make him hers. She pivoted her hips up to take more of him inside her, his movements sure against her pelvis. He thrust in and let her squirm on his sword. She felt his the base of his shaft hard against her sex. He moaned this time as she wiggled, in little circles, stimulating herself.

Kelly couldn't believe she already felt her need rising in her again. She wanted to feel him deeper within her, need making her clench tight. The resounding response to her spasms was a thickening of his shaft. She felt him strain against her, sliding in and out, in a growing rhythm. She knew he would cum soon. She begged him, with her soft moans to release both of them. He slammed into her one last time, pressing all the way into her as he pulsed with his release. She arched with him and the glorious glow of a second orgasm washed over her.

Jack, spent, relaxed and let his weight settle on top of her. They were both breathing fast. He looked into her eyes and found her soul. "I love you," he whispered with all his heart behind the words. "I will never let you go." There was so much more that he wanted to say, but he couldn't find the words. He leaned over to show her with his kisses.

Kelly floated in a heavenly haze. Jack interrupted her drifting. "I love you," he said and she held her breath as he finished, "Will you marry me?" Rising up over her, he leaned down to kiss her mouth, gently, lovingly. She knew it was true; that he loved her. She loved him just as deeply.

"Yes. Yes, I'll marry you." Tears welled in her eyes and she looked away from him to hide them, lest he not understand. Her gaze fell on her surroundings. Her eyes had adjusted enough to recognize a few things in the room. With rising horror she saw the chair she had been tied to and the stove that was radiating heat.

Jack thought he saw tears in Kelly's eyes, but she turned her head away from him so he wasn't sure. Suddenly Kelly's body jerked rigid under his touch. She sat up pushing Jack off of her, "We have to get out of here! This is Albert's cabin. We aren't safe here!"

Jack soothed, "it's okay, he's dead. He can't bother you again." Jack followed his reassurance with a firm pressure on her chest and his lips on hers. They fell back into bed, back into bliss.

Jack held her while she snuggled into his shoulder. The feeling to protect her overwhelmed him. He loved her so much. As her breathing quieted he knew he would work the rest of his life to show her how much she meant to him. They would just have to deal with the police department rules later. Right now they had a few days, while they were snowed in, to connect.

I hope you enjoyed reading Tender Bait as much as I enjoyed writing it. If you could take a few moments to write a nice review on Amazon or other booksellers, I would really appreciate it.

— Lara